SUMMER OF SURPRISE

SUMME

OF SURPRISE

by Helen Reynolds

FUNK & WAGNALLS COMPANY • NEW YORK

to
Muriel Fuller

Contents

SUMMER OF SURPRISE

1

Orchard Home

We were all making plans for the summer while we packed the works of art we had wrought during the previous ten months, and at the same time we were turning backward glances at the good times we had had in the School of Art. I was taking home a table runner I had woven, several pieces of pottery, a framed picture in petit point, and a number of smaller items—all of my own design. I, Penelope Warburton, was looking forward to a busy summer in my dad's orchard, with time out for riding, tennis, and swimming. At the same time I hated to leave the work I loved and the grand friends I had made in three years.

Visitors to the School of Art raised their eyebrows at some of the boys who grew fuzzy beards and wore berets or wide-brimmed hats and tried to look like artists on the Left Bank in Paris, while they argued loudly about Cézanne, Picasso, or Dégas and scoffed at the Pre-Raphaelites and Impressionists. Our boys carried on like this about experimental art, but under all their nonsense they were keen students and fun to know. The girls were good pals, and full of original ideas.

In my first and second years at art school I had taken courses in drawing, painting, and design. After that I had to choose fine art, commercial art, or crafts. I love to make useful things, so I decided on the crafts.

"I wish you weren't going out of town," Sybil Coates said. "We could have such fun this summer, sketching all over the place, swimming and sailing. My brother has a Star, and he'd take us out sometimes."

Sailing! How I loved it! I could swim and dive at Kelowna, but I had no friend there who owned a sailboat. "If I were twins," I replied. "I'm just about split in two, crazy to go home, and hating to leave school. Never mind, it's only for two months; I'll be back in September."

If only I could have looked in a crystal ball!

"What will you do with yourself, out in the sticks?" Joan Mackay asked. Joan is one of those intense artists. She eats her meals with a brush in her hand. She simply can't figure anyone who wants to be an artist doing such things as I would be doing, so I kind of hedged.

"Oh, there's plenty of activity even in the sticks."

"But what exactly? I'm trying to picture you in a strange, wild environment. Tell me all you do."

She was looking at me with big dark eyes full of earnest probing, so I had to satisfy her. I was tempted to sell her a line of goods, but her pure, intense gaze demanded the truth, the whole truth, and nothing but the truth.

"The first thing will be picking cherries, and in the evenings I'll be helping my mother to process dozens of bottles of fruit and jam too. There'll be early apples to pick."

"Do you work *all* the time?" Joan demanded, frowning. "Don't you have any time for painting, or doing designs for your craft work?"

She took off her smock, which was itself like an abstract painting, covered with daubs of paint, clay, and glaze. I hated to lose face with her, but I answered defiantly, "I don't suppose I'll have time to pick up a pencil, or model a small bowl."

Little did I know!

"I don't want you to think my parents are slave-drivers," I added quickly. "I'll ride my palomino and go picnicking and swimming, and to a few dances, I hope. I have a friend who has a tennis court, and we play. There'll be the Kelowna Regatta, which draws tourists from all over, and later a gymkhana. Oh, we have heaps of fun in the Valley."

"Hmph!" was all Joan deigned to reply. She considered that I was not making a noise like an artist.

I was sorry to lose Joan's good opinion, but I had to tell the truth—what I in my happy ignorance believed to be the truth—about my summer's activities.

I would have traveled by bus, since it was more economical than Pullman or plane, but I had such ungainly baggage that I decided to go by train. I could leave in the evening, sleep some, I hoped, and reach Kelowna in the middle of the morning. So I bought a ticket and checked my suitcases and my trunk full of art supplies and craft pieces. Dad and my young brother Eric met me at the depot and carried my suitcases to the old Ford.

"I'll have to pick up your trunk when I'm in with the truck," Dad said.

It was lovely to see Dad, and Eric seemed more human

than he had been when I went away. I thought Dad looked older than I remembered him. Soon we were in the car and rumbling along the road to the KLO bench. In the Okanagan Valley the land is laid out in plateaux, called benches, one beyond and higher than another. Our home, The Poplars, is on the first, the KLO bench, and we go from the flat valley up a winding road to an equally flat bench, where the road runs straight as a T square, with orchards on either side. It was too late for the sweetness of apple blossoms and the bright faces of balsamroot sunflowers around every fence post, but I sniffed the sagebrush and knew that I was in my own country.

As we drove along, I could feel the springs coming through the stuffing of the seat, and there were clanks and rattles that sounded as if the Ford were near its doom.

"Dad," I grumbled, "how long are you going to drive this old heap? It will suddenly disintegrate, like the Deacon's One-Hoss Shay, and spill you out on the road."

"There's life in the old bus yet," Dad growled. "It wouldn't bring in ten dollars on a trade-in, and it isn't convenient for me to buy another just now."

"Have the cherries set well?" I asked. "No splitting?"

"A good crop," he said, "praises be. Last year wasn't so good."

"I can hardly wait to see Mother. Why didn't she come too?"

"She thought your baggage would take all the room."

Dad turned out to pass an older car than his own, a pick-up truck loaded with junk, driven by an ancient Chinese. I waved to him as we passed. "Hello, Wong Kee!"

I turned to Dad. "I have a jar of ginger for Wong Kee in my trunk. Whatever does he do with all that junk?"

"He trades, and he mends things," Dad explained. "He

says he's saving money to bring his grandson over from China."

"I see he has a sewing machine this trip," I observed, never dreaming how that sewing machine would enter my life.

We turned off the straight road and drove through the orchard to the house. As I got out of the car Mac, our collie, came bounding to meet me, jumping and trying to lick my face. And there was my dear mother coming out of the wide, screened veranda. We hugged and kissed.

"Well, how is our young artist?" She held me off and looked at me keenly. "You're thin, dear. Have you been working too hard? Or not eating proper meals?"

"I'm fine, Mother. Only a little bit tired. We had to work for the final exhibition and then clear things up and pack, and I didn't sleep well last night."

We went into the house. The original owner of The Poplars had had English ideas and also a large family to find room for. He had built the type of house he had owned in England. The dining room was large enough for at least twenty-four to sit down to a meal, and the drawing room was forty feet long. We didn't have enough furniture for such a room, so we had made the dining room into a comfortable living room. We had our meals on the veranda in the long, hot summers and in the warm kitchen in winter. Only at Christmas did we decorate the large room and set up the tree there. On New Year's Eve some of our friends always came in, and we waxed the floor for dancing.

Dad and Eric carried my suitcases up to my room. Mother had washed and starched the dotted-muslin curtains at my window, and the room looked so spotless and neat that I was almost afraid to unpack my suitcases and strew things about. Every year when I come home I find my room immaculate; every year I resolve to keep it neat; every year it quickly gets to look as though a tornado had struck it. I can't understand what happens.

"I hope the truck will soon be going into town," I told my mother, "because I have presents for you in my trunk, and I can hardly wait to show you what I designed and made at school."

"Oh, lovely!" she cried. "I'm longing to see your work. I'll coax your father to make the trip this afternoon. I don't know why he didn't take the truck this morning. You and Eric could have squeezed into the cab with him."

It was lunch time then, and Mother had made a cherry pie in my honor. Then, when Dad was feeling pleasantly satisfied, Mother said she was crazy to see the work Penelope had brought home. Dad gave a sort of agreeable grunt.

"That means I must drive into town for the trunk, I suppose. However, I can probably combine the trip with some business in order to soothe my conscience."

How we talked!—or, rather, how *I* talked!—all through lunch and while I helped Mother with the dishes. I had so much to tell them that I didn't realize how little they told me. Eric, of course, had just one topic of conversation—cars, and especially a Model-A he bought for ten dollars, which he was slowly taking to pieces and putting together again with parts from the junk yard.

Then I went to visit my horse Goldie in the pasture. Goldie is a beautiful palomino, bright as his name. He knew my voice and came trotting to the fence, tossing his silver mane and tail. I wasn't dressed for riding, but, when I had given him a lump of sugar, I couldn't resist coaxing him close to the fence and climbing from the top rail onto his back. He was fat and smooth as a cushion from loafing in the pasture and doing no work. I didn't need bit or bridle to ride him around the pasture because he has been trained to obey hand signals.

"You'll need some good hard exercise, my boy, if you're going to be fit to enter the gymkhana in August," I told him. I could feel that he was soft and out of condition. It was a hot day, and he was sweating lightly in a few minutes of cantering around the pasture.

It was good to be home, I thought. Oh, it was very good to be home. The air was so fresh and sweet, the smokeless sky so blue. After my short ride I walked through the orchard and saw how well laden with green apples all the trees were. The Royal Anne cherries were ripe, and I picked a handful to eat as I went. A hen pheasant was leading a family of downy chicks under the trees. Pheasants are the most casual of mothers. They are quite likely to lay a clutch of eggs in a hollow in the ground and then go off and lay another clutch somewhere else.

"I must ride over and visit Diana," I said to myself.

I ran back to the house to change into a white blouse and jodhpurs. "Mother," I called out, "I'm going to ride over and say hello to Diana."

"Don't be late for tea," she warned. "Dad will have your trunk here, and we'll all be biting our fingers to the bone with impatience."

"I won't be late," I promised. I was out of the house in a minute and back to the pasture with a bridle. It was no trick at all to catch Goldie and put the bridle on. He was so gentle and willing that I didn't have to rattle a pan of oats or hold the bridle behind my back. I led him to the stable and saddled him, mounted, and rode away.

From the rim of the second bench I could look over Okanagan Lake, miles away, a band of silver lying along the feet of the delft-blue range beyond. To the north the flat valley stretched for miles, walled in by humpy hills of sand and sagebrush, sparsely timbered, and far-off green mountains. I drew rein and gazed and loved it all.

Soon I came to the Truscotts' land and stopped at Diana's home, a modern ranch house set in a glowing garden. Her mother came to the door.

"I'm glad to see you home, Penelope, dear," she greeted me. "I'm sorry Diana isn't here. She's picking cherries a mile from here. Won't you come in and have a glass of fruit juice? Diana will be so sorry she missed you. I'm sure she'll drive over to see you in the evening."

"I think I won't stop now, thank you, Mrs. Truscott," I answered. "Mother told me to be home in time for tea. Give my love to Diana. I do hope she'll come over this evening."

I was disappointed, but I rode home faster, longing to open my trunk and give my presents to the family. I passed cherry orchards where crews of girls were at work. They wore gaily colored kerchiefs around their heads to protect their hair from catching in the branches, and as they poked out among the leaves they looked like a flock of parrots. Some of them saw me and called out, "Hi, Penelope! Glad to see you back." That was all that was needed to make me feel that I had come home to the valley.

I turned Goldie loose in the pasture and went into the house to change back into a dress. I found Mother taking the tea tray out to the veranda. Dad and Eric had carried my trunk up to my room. I couldn't wait to open it and bring down my best pieces to show and to give to my mother. The woven table runner, a vase, and the petit point picture were for her and leather work for the men. I was saving my other pieces for Christmas gifts.

"These are really lovely, Penelope," Mother said. "I shall

treasure them. You are truly artistic, dear. I don't know how you get that way. Dad and I are so humdrum."

She poured me a cup of tea, and I was glad to see a plate of ranch-style raisin bread in good thick slices. I was hungry after my ride.

"Your own original designs, girlie," Dad said admiringly. "Very clever."

"I have a leather billfold for you and a key case for Eric." As I handed them, I apologized, "I haven't done much leather work yet."

Dad was ridiculously pleased; his bald spot grew quite pink. Eric made suitable noises to show that he was gratified. Eric is quite inarticulate except when he is talking about valves, carbureters, ignition, piston rings, and things like that. I guess all teen-age boys are the same—car-crazy.

"You certainly are generous, darling, giving all your choice pieces to your family," Mother said. "I hope you've kept some for yourself. Some day you'll have your own home to display them in."

"I've kept some to give to Grannie and the aunts at Christmas," I told her. "I'll show them to you next time I go to my room. I can make things for myself. Next year at art school I shall make heaps of things."

There was an uncomfortable silence. I saw Dad glance at Mother and saw her slight nod, and I wondered unhappily what I had done wrong. Dad coughed. He took his pipe out of his pocket and stuffed it with tobacco.

"I had intended to let you have this first day without any worries or bad news, dear," he said slowly, "but I may as well tell you. I'm afraid you'll have to skip art school next fall. I took a beating on last year's apple crop. In fact, I lost seventy-nine cents on every box of apples I shipped, and that pretty well cleaned me out. I've been able to squeeze

enough out of my bank manager to carry on until the
cherry crop is paid for, but we'll have to cut out the frills
entirely."

It knocked the wind out of me. I felt sick. I had expected
that I would finish school and get my diploma just the way
I expected the sun to rise tomorrow. In apple growing there
were good years and bad years, and it wasn't the first time
Dad had taken a beating and recovered. But why, oh, why
did it have to be this time when I could have won mv
diploma and been eligible for a job?

"Oh, Daddy, dear, I'm sorry. I shouldn't have taken a
berth in the train," was all I could think of to say.

"Nonsense! We're not so broke as that yet." Dad patted
my shoulder. "There's a big difference between a Pullman
and a year at the art school. I can't tell you how sorry I am
about this, old girl."

"I think I'll go and finish unpacking when I've taken the
tea things out," I said. I could feel the tears coming.

2

Frustration

All the joy had gone out of my home-coming. It seemed as if my plans for a career were shattered. Without a diploma I could never get a position as occupational therapist in a hospital or as a designer in a factory as I had hoped. I carried in the tray of empty cups and washed them, all the time not speaking, because I was stunned. A few tears fell in the dish water. I couldn't think or see ahead. Mother came out to the kitchen.

"This is a blow to you and a setback, dear." She put her arms around my shoulders. "But it's not the end of everything. In a year or two things may be better, and you'll be able to complete your training. This has been pretty hard on your father, too, and on me."

Those few words were a flashlight turned on my selfishness, and I was ashamed. "I'll get some kind of job that will help us all," I assured my mother, though actually I didn't have a clew.

"Brave girl! Brave words!" Mother gave me a little pat.

I had been intending to go up to my room and have a good howl, but now I pulled myself together and made up my mind to be brave, boo-hoo, a sweet, brave daughter. I was so noble and saintly that I was funny, and suddenly I had to laugh at myself.

Mother peered at me anxiously, as though she thought I was hysterical. "Why do you laugh, dear? A minute ago you looked as though you'd never laugh again."

"I guess I was laughing at myself for making a tragedy out of a disappointment. We'll muddle through."

That evening Diana drove over in her father's new Dodge. I was thrilled to see her and have a good old talk fest. I took her up to my room, where we could yaketty-yak without disturbing the adults. After we had told each other every single thing that had happened while I was away, I got round to my fresh trouble and problem. I was a little bit chilled by Diana's unconcern. She stood in front of my mirror, trying on my earrings, and seemed hardly to listen.

"All the apple growers took a loss last year," she told me calmly. "My dad lost money. He couldn't have bought a new car if he hadn't sold a lot of bonds or something."

"I haven't a lot of bonds or something to sell," I mentioned, "and I'm trying to dream up some way to earn money to help out and maybe even to put me through next year."

"Can't you pick cherries and thin apples like the rest of us?" Diana asked. "Why are you so set on another year of art school? You've had three, haven't you? Why don't you just stay home?"

"I have to get my diploma or bang goes my chance of a job."

"Oh, *that!*" she brushed it off. "You can always make

enough to buy your own clothes by picking and packing fruit, and then you'll probably get married."

I didn't say a word. Diana and I had been chums for eight years, and now suddenly we were strangers. We could yak about clothes and parties and boy friends and all the things that don't matter, but the subject of art was like a room in which I lived alone and Diana stayed outside of her own free will. I felt terribly lonesome.

"Let's go down and make some lemonade," I suggested, jumping up, "or would you prefer coffee?"

"A cup of coffee would be fine," Diana said. "I was up with the meadowlarks this morning. Coffee will keep me awake to drive home. Are you going to train Goldie for the gymkhana this year?"

"I don't know whether I'll have time," I temporized.

So we went down, still talking, and I made coffee for everyone, and cut cake, and sounded happy and gay, and all the time I was mad clear through. I was mad because I was in a tough spot and no one was giving a thought to helping me out of it. I was so mad that I gritted my teeth and vowed I'd find a way out for myself.

Diana's people have plenty of money, and Diana's own face is her fortune. She is pretty, with dark eyes and hair, a beautiful mouth, and a creamy complexion. She can afford to stay home until she marries, and she can marry whenever she makes up her mind among her admirers.

No one can say whether I'm pretty or not, because my face is never still long enough to tell what I look like. Dad calls it my "infinite variety," and Mother says my face is too expressive and tells tales when I don't like people. One of my teachers said I had an interesting face and tried to draw my portrait. No luck. I am thin and springy. My face is usually tanned brown and my hair bleached almost white by the hot sun of the valley. And that's enough about me.

"It's grand to have you home again, Pen," Diana said, standing up, lovely and graceful. "You'll have to come over to dinner soon. We can play tennis in the evening. Some of the boys always come over."

"I'd love to," I said. Diana is a tournament tennis player. When we play doubles, I'm given the strongest boy as a partner to even things up. I went out with her and admired the new Dodge, and she got in and drove away.

That night I could not sleep. The country noises were different from the city noises; the night was warm and I kept turning my pillow over; my brain was fussing around trying to find an idea for making money, much more money than I could make by picking fruit. I should have remembered what coffee does to me.

In the valley it is never quite dark in summer. Around the ranges that wall us in there is always a faint light. I've heard the scientific name for it, but I forget what it is. The light of dawn was just beginning to brighten this earth light when I had an idea. I had a kiln in the basement. Why shouldn't I make pottery with fruit designs and sell it to the tourists at good prices? There had been such things on the market. Why not do some original, striking designs? I was sure I could. I relaxed then, went to sleep, and slept until noon.

When I looked at my watch, I was horrified, and I can tell you I bounced out of bed in a hurry. Spending half the night planning to be a help, and then sleeping until the middle of the day! What a gal! I had a quick bath for fear the pressure should be low by evening. I remembered the KLO water problem. I hustled into a blouse and shorts and ran downstairs.

"Well, darling," Mother said, all smiles, "I'm glad you had a good, long sleep. I hope you feel rested."

"I feel terrible, sleeping late when I intended to help you," I confessed. "I didn't get to sleep until nearly getting-up time. I was trying to dope out a plan to earn money, lots of money, and help Dad out of the red."

Mother looked really interested. "And did you think of a plan?"

"I got a sort of germ of an idea. I remembered my kiln in the basement, and I wondered if I could design pottery and make it to sell to tourists."

"That has been done successfully," Mother reminded me. "You would have to make a totally new design, something very attractive."

"I would make a new, attractive design. I know I can. I believe I could make all sorts of craft work, woven stuff and leather work. Surely, after three years of art-school training I should be able to design and make items that would sell as gifts or tourist bait."

"It would be a venture," Mother said. "On the other hand, you can be sure of wages all through the fruit season."

"I'll pick in the daytime and model and weave in the evenings," I said. "That sort of work is pleasure to me, and I'll get my fresh air and exercise working in the orchards."

Mother shook her head doubtfully. "I don't want you to wear yourself out, child."

"I'm strong as a horse," I boasted. "I had been planning to help you can fruit in the evenings. I said to one of the girls at school that I wished I was twins, and now I wish it more than ever."

Mother laughed. "If you were twins, you would eat

twice as much, wear twice as many clothes, and need two diplomas, so I don't think you'd gain much."

Dad came in to lunch then, and I asked him if I could start work picking cherries.

"I have a crew coming tomorrow," he said. "I'd really prefer to have you thin apples. You can start on the Macs, keep your time, and I'll pay you wages when I can."

"I don't want you to pay me wages, thank you, Dad."

"Oh, yes, you do. Keep your time," Dad insisted.

I was disappointed that I could not pick cherries with a crew of girls I knew. Also, green apples are not good to eat.

Before I started thinning apples, I went down to the basement room to look at my kiln. It was cached away in a corner, covered with dust and cobwebs. I cleaned it off and made sure that the electric connection was in good order. There were shelves and a table, and I could see myself working in a cool place in the heat of summer. I also found that I had a good stock of clay in a large tin container and a small amount of the red clay from the northern part of the province that bakes to a beautiful rich brown.

Feeling happier, I tied a kerchief around my head and went out to find a ladder. I took one of the short, light ladders that the girls use and put it up in the first tree of the nearest row.

"Thinning apples," I muttered, "and me with a cherry thirst, and all those luscious Royal Annes hanging in bunches."

I thinned apples until Mother called me in for a cup of tea and then went on thinning until six. I knew I should see thousands of little green apples in my dreams because that's the way thinning always affects me. While I worked, I was thinking about designs for pottery and trying to make up my mind whether to make vases or cream-and-sugar sets. Would cake plates have a better sale? I was beginning to have doubts about the whole venture.

That evening I mixed some clay and wedged it by throwing it on a canvas mat to drive out the air bubbles. Then I molded a jug. It was good to feel the moist clay in my fingers once again. One of my teachers had preferred the coil system of building a piece; another had modeled out of a rounded lump. I had been taught to use a template and a potter's wheel. I didn't have a template or a potter's wheel, so I just molded the jug as if it were a large pinch pot.

On my way to the laundry stand tubs to wash the clay off my fingers I ran into my dear little brother.

"Hi, Pen," he said, grinning. "Been making mud pies? Second childhood coming on?"

"I've made a cream jug, that's all," I said casually.

"For your hope chest, I'll bet."

"I do not possess a hope chest." I was very lofty. "I intend to be a career woman."

"What sort of career woman?"

Now my ideas hadn't quite jelled yet about what sort of career, so I said shortly, "A useful career, I hope."

"I don't see much future in making cream jugs all your life," Eric scoffed. "I should think you'd want to paint stage scenery or make statues or something like that. Something big."

Why do boys have to be like that? I went to the stand tubs and turned on a tap. There was not a trickle of water.

When I had had my bath in the morning, I had recollected that little peculiarity of the water system on the benches, but in the meantime it had slipped my mind. It doesn't happen often, though, even in hot weather. So there was I with my hands covered with damp clay rapidly cak-

ing on them. I went out to the horse trough, which was
filled with clean, cold water. Goldie had been watered, and
there was no other stock to consider, so I rinsed my hands
in that and hoped Mother had saved some in jugs before
the pressure went off.

I had been so hot all day that I wanted a second bath. It
was not really dark, and Mission Creek was only a mile
away. I went to my room and put on my bathing suit and
my shirt and shorts over it. Out I went to the harness room,
picked Goldie's bridle off its peg, and went out to the pasture. Goldie was excited at being taken for a run in the
dusk, and in ten minutes we were at the bridge across the
creek, on the road that leads toward Black Mountain and
the Belgo lands.

I tied Goldie to a tree, and in a minute I was splashing in
the cold water of the creek. It certainly was cold, and there
were cobblestones underfoot. It was pretty rough, but it
was clean and wet, and pretty soon I was clean and wet
too.

It was a little eerie in the darkness of the poplars and
aspens. All the sounds were softened by the creek burbling
over the stones—Goldie stamping restlessly, birds rustling
in the trees with sleepy twitterings, small animals moving,
coyotes howling in the distance. I was glad to be riding
home, facing the last gleam in the western sky. That night
I slept so soundly that I didn't even dream of little green
apples.

Next day I thinned apples for eight hours. Though I was
tired after dinner, I made myself go down to the basement
and model a sugar bowl to go with my jug. I still had to
make up my mind about glazing and decorating my pottery. I felt like drawing a design of little green apples, but I

knew tourists wouldn't understand. They like their apples round and red.

I was just finishing the small bowl when I heard voices coming down the basement stairs. Eric was bringing someone to visit me or perhaps to see his car parts. In any case, they would be curious and want to see what I was doing, and I was not pleased, because my pottery was still in the experimental stage.

"Hi, Penelope!" cried a voice I knew well.

"Hi, Lyn! How's life treating you?"

Lyn Brown's father owned a large cherry orchard next to ours. Lyn was fifteen, a shy, eager girl, given to baseless enthusiasms.

"What are you doing?" she asked inevitably. "Are you making a clay thing? Oh, a bowl. Isn't that a cute shape? Is it for sugar? Are you going to make a jug to go with it?"

She rattled off the questions so fast I had no chance to answer until the last. "I've made a jug. It's drying, but I have to bake them both."

"In your kiln? What fun! Oh, Penelope, will you teach me to make pottery? My dad would be willing to pay for lessons. He'd be glad to. He often says he wishes I'd do something useful in the evenings instead of watching TV all the time."

"Don't you have any homework?" I asked.

"Not in the summer vacation. You know that, Penelope."

A new idea was coming to the boil in my mind. If I could gather a few pupils, I might be teaching while I was making pottery myself and bring in extra dollars that way.

"I'd like to teach you, Lyn," I said, "but I'd have to consult my father first. I'll let you know in a day or two."

I wedged a lump of clay for her to play with so that she

could get the feeling of it in her fingers. She was en-
chanted.

"It's more fun than plasticine," she said. "When I was a
kid, I always loved to play with plasticine and modeling
clay."

When you were a kid, I thought. What are you now?

"I bet Susan would like to have lessons too." Lyn's enthusiasm extended to her friend. "If you were teaching one,
it wouldn't be too much trouble to teach Susan, too, would
it? Do you have enough clay for two pupils?"

"I have a hundred pounds of powdered clay I've just
started on," I laughed. "I don't think we'll use that up in a
hurry."

We went up to the living room and found my father.
"Dad," I said, "we want your advice. Lyn would like me to
teach her to model in clay, and she would pay for lessons.
Maybe Susan would come, too. Would that be OK?"

"Sure," Dad answered in a surprised tone of voice. He
hadn't realized that I was capable of teaching a craft. "It's
up to you, girlie, if you want to give lessons."

"I'll have to charge a dollar an hour," I told Lyn, hoping
it didn't sound too much. "Let me know what your father
says about it."

Lyn went home, bubbling with enthusiasm. I roamed
around the house. Ideas were floating about in my head,
trying to fit themselves into a pattern. Possibly someone
would like to learn to weave. There were my large loom
and my cradle loom standing lonely in the big empty drawing room that we only use in the Christmas holidays. What
a splendid classroom it would make!

I went in and looked around. I could teach pottery up
here as well as weaving and maybe leather work. I should
need a big table and some stools or plain chairs and mat-

ting to protect the floor. I believed I could find those items around the house or buy them cheap from Wong Kee. If I had five or six pupils, it would be worthwhile fixing the place up as a studio.

3

The Venture

After Lyn had gone home with the good news and I had
started to dream of a class of five or six pupils, I opened the
windows to air the large room. It had the peculiar smell of
a room shut up for months. A few fir needles from the
Christmas tree still lay on the floor. I brought a dust mop
and went over the waxed floor and dusted my large loom.
If I brought in the ping-pong table from the veranda, I
could use it for clay modeling. Somehow, I should have to
scrounge a mat or canvas to protect the hardwood floor.

There was no doubt I could make it into a first-class
workroom, but the question was whether I could attract
enough pupils to make my time worthwhile. I could make
good wages by picking fruit. Would teaching crafts pay
better? The world wasn't filled with Lyn Browns, bubbling
like a tea kettle and sending out a steam of enthusiasm. I'd
have to sleep on it and consult Mother and Dad.

By this time they had gone to bed, so I had to leave my

problem for the morning. But I could see the whole plan plainly—two pupils weaving on the two looms, three or four around the table, working with clay, and myself at one end of the table, demonstrating. My demonstration pieces I would decorate and glaze for sale. I was so thrilled that I hated to go to sleep without finding an audience for my grand scheme. Perhaps Mother and Dad aren't asleep yet, I hoped. I listened at their door. Dad was sleeping like a saw going through a knotty log, so I toddled off to bed.

At breakfast next morning everyone was in a hurry to go off to work, and it was no time to talk of dreams, so I went out reluctantly to thin those darned little apples. I had my chance later as we were relaxing after dinner.

"I have an idea in my mind, Dad," I began diffidently. "I hope it won't sound too screwy to you. There's my kiln in the basement, and my looms are in the drawing room, and there's Lyn clamoring for lessons. Do you suppose I could take some pupils and at the same time make pottery and things to sell in a gift shop?"

Three pairs of eyes widened at the idea of my presuming to start a class. Eric, the darling, was the first to speak.

"Getting tired of thinning apples, huh?"

"That is quite uncalled for, Eric." Mother put him in his place. "Penelope's idea has much in its favor . . . provided that she can get the pupils."

"I'll give you this bit of advice," Dad said. "Don't charge by the single lesson. They miss a lesson and waste your time waiting for them and think they don't have to pay. Have a series of lessons for a price, whether they choose to come or not. If you yourself should be ill or unable to take the class, remit a certain amount or give an extra lesson later. My sister gave music lessons at so much a lesson. Some days her pupils would have some other attraction and stay away without a word, leaving her to waste *her* time without pay."

"That's the best plan," Mother agreed. "If they're paying a flat sum for the course, they'll do their best to come."

I didn't like that idea much. I should hate to take money without giving value, but I could see that by giving a course at a lower rate than a dollar a lesson I could come out better if pupils missed lessons, and they could come out better if they showed up regularly.

"Do you think I should advertise in the local papers?" I asked.

"Hm-m." Dad stroked his chin thoughtfully.

I could see that Dad didn't like the notion of advertising craft teaching before I had gained my diploma. The same objection was in my mind, and it pinpointed my need of a diploma.

"Shall we see if Lyn comes back with her father's consent and possibly brings Susan Brown to make a throng of two," Mother suggested.

"That's a good plan," Dad said heartily.

Again my incorrigible young brother put in his oar. "Dad is glad to pass the buck," he remarked with a grin.

Dad frowned at him. "Nothing of the sort, young man. I merely think it wise for Penelope to feel her way and not jump with both feet into a situation that . . . a situation that . . ."

Suddenly we all began to laugh. No one can be serious for long in this family, and most of our tiffs and worries seem to pass off in a breeze of laughter.

"OK, we'll see if Lyn shows up," I agreed.

At that very moment we saw Lyn coming up the road, towing Susan. Susan is plump and lazy, and her wide blue eyes have about as much expression as a doll's. It's hard to fathom Lyn's need of her, unless Susan acts as a sponge to soak up the overflow of Lyn's vitality. They came to the screened veranda, where I was picking up the dessert plates to carry them into the kitchen.

"Dad says I can have lessons," Lyn said breathlessly, "and Susan doesn't want to come, but I told her, when she sees the things you've made, she'll want to make some, too."

"I don't like messing in mud," Susan said. "I'm too old for mud pies, but I wouldn't mind learning to weave. If it's like making paper mats in kindergarten, it's pretty easy I guess."

"You're not any older than I am, Susan," Lyn said, "and anyway, Mrs. Bellair said she'd like to learn to make pottery, and she's terribly old. I bet she's fifty. I don't know what use she thinks it would be to learn anything at *her* age."

"So Mrs. Bellair is interested," I said. "I can't teach you to model in the basement and at the same time teach Susan to weave in the drawing room . . ." I started to object, with a hopeful eye on Mother.

Mother played up as I had hoped. "There's a square of floor covering in the attic that you could lay on a part of the drawing-room floor. You may bring in the ping-pong table from the veranda, and we can round up some chairs and stools and a small table or two. Then you can teach both girls in the same place."

"Can I have a lesson right now, and Susan watch to see if she likes it?" Lyn asked. Her fingers were twining and twisting with energy going to waste.

"I'll help Mum with the dishes," Eric offered.

"Yes, dear," Mother added. "Don't wait till the iron cools."

I took the girls down to the basement room and mixed some clay. I showed Lyn how to wedge a lump of clay and make a pinch pot. Susan watched with casual curiosity. I molded a saucer to go with my cream and sugar, intending to make a cup when I had taken time to design a shape.

"Isn't it fun, Susan?" Lyn demanded. "Isn't this a cute little pinch pot? Oh, gosh, I've broken the edge. What shall I do now?"

I made some slip with clay and water and mended the pinch pot for her. Soon we were having a marvelous time. I hadn't been sure that I could pass on what I had learned. I found that I liked to teach. It seemed that this knowledge and skill that I had spent three years to acquire ought to be shared. Susan's doll eyes began to show a gleam of interest.

"Would you like a lump of clay to play with?" I asked her.

"I don't mind if I do," she said flatly.

She made a little pig, like a piggy bank. "It's kind of fun," she admitted. "I don't get my hands too messy. I guess I'll take clay modeling as well as weaving."

"Mrs. Bellair is coming to see you," Susan said. "She told my mother that she needs a hobby, and she thinks making pottery is just what she'd like, only she called it a fancy name I can't remember."

"Ceramics," I suggested.

"Yes, that was the word, cermarics."

"Ceramics," I corrected, but to the end of the course Susan persisted in calling it "cermarics."

Inwardly I quaked at the thought of having Mrs. Bellair as a pupil. She has a large estate with an apple orchard, stables for polo ponies, and a nine-hole golf course. She is fussy and self-important and accustomed to ordering people around. I just couldn't see myself telling Mrs. Bellair that her modeling wasn't perfect. If I shut my eyes, I could see her, short and thin, very upright, in tweeds and a floppy hat, with pearls . . . real ones . . . around her sinewy throat and great diamonds and rubies on her thin hands.

I arranged with the girls for their next lesson and sent them off so that they would be home before dark. Then I went to my room and took pencil and paper to design the shape of my cup and the decoration. Should it be apples, cherries, balsamroot sunflowers, or a stylized Ogopogo, the lake monster that is seen at times and has become a legend?

Other private ceramic concerns had made pottery decorated with fruit, so I decided to try the Ogopogo, which is a tourist attraction. I could make the coils of it curling around cups and bowls. Having never seen the creature myself, I was able to give my imagination full play. I did several drawings of cups before I was satisfied with a shape. Then I started drawing decorative Ogopogos. I have heard the monster described as being forty or fifty feet long, with a head like a horse or like a sheep with a mane. How in the world could I make this weird thing look decorative?

How should I plan my teaching? Should I or should I not do it in a big way and have a summer school of arts and crafts? I didn't know whether I could swing anything as big as that. However, I didn't stand to lose much except my time, because I already had the classroom and a good deal of equipment.

The cold truth was I was scared of Mrs. Bellair. Would she drive me nuts and make it hard to handle the teenagers? I went to bed when I was too tired to draw the Ogopogo, and I was still in a dither.

First thing in the morning a telephone call helped me to make up my mind. "This is Mrs. Terry. May I speak to

Penelope? Oh, it's you, Penelope. I hear you're giving lessons in pottery and weaving. I should love it if you would
take Pat for three hours five times a week. He's so lonely
and bored. I'm sure it would be a great help to him."

Pat Terry is lame and spends most of his time in a wheel-
chair, although he can walk in a slow shuffle. He is in his
early twenties. I couldn't refuse to help a man who was dis-
abled and bored. I hoped to make a career of teaching pa-
tients in some hospital, so why not start now?

"That will be lovely, Mrs. Terry," I answered. "It will
take me all of today to get the studio ready for work. Would
Pat be coming in the morning or the afternoon?"

"From one to four," Mrs. Terry said without hesitation,
just as if she were giving the course, not I. "I will bring
him in the car and pick him up at four. You will be stopping for tea then, anyway."

She didn't even bother to ask about my fee. That settled
it. I must decide on a definite course of lessons and a fee
and then advertise, either in the local press, by fliers, or by
the good old moccasin telegraph. In the country the party
line could be counted on to spread the news, but I must
have a definite prospectus.

The first thing was to turn the empty drawing room into
a studio. Eric suddenly turned angel and was eager to help.
We put down an old square of linoleum and a strip of canvas for wedging clay. Then we carried in the ping-pong table and scrubbed it.

"We need a low table and a comfortable chair for Pat
Terry," I said. "I can give up the low chair and a cushion
from my room, but where is there a table?"

"There's a table in the attic," Eric recalled. "I can saw off
the legs."

There were empty bookshelves against one wall that

would do to stand pottery on to dry. We brought up the clay and some empty cans from the basement. "We should have stools to sit on beside the table," I said.

"I'll try Wong Kee." Eric shot off and soon came back with a stool.

"Wong Kee says there are some old stools in the cherry-packing shed. There's a can of blue paint in the toolshed. We can paint them."

I brought down my tools: my brass-wire clay cutter, scrapers, knife, and pieces of leather and felt for smoothing. I coaxed a white enamel basin from Mother.

I decided to offer a course of nineteen lessons for fifteen dollars. That would take me to the end of July, and then, if it proved a success, I could offer a second course. Each lesson would be for three hours, and the course would be for five days a week. In that way I could find room for six pupils in the morning and six in the afternoon. That would give me one hundred and eighty dollars. I had it all worked out on paper, and I was so excited that I had put Mrs. Bellair out of my mind. I was taking a big leap in the dark, and I had no idea where I would land.

On Sunday when I came out of church, Mrs. Bellair was waiting for me. "I never talk business on Sunday," she said, "but I want to see you. Will you be at home tomorrow morning, or will you be up a cherry tree?"

"I shall be at home, Mrs. Bellair," I said, "getting ready for craft lessons that I shall be teaching in the afternoon. I'll be glad to show you my studio."

"Splendid," she said. "I'll drop in some time during the morning."

In the morning I telephoned to Mrs. Brown and Mrs. Smither and told them my plan and my charge. They both agreed to send the girls to the morning class.

"If they'll hop right over," I said, "we can start today."

So, when Mrs. Bellair came in, there was my school in session, although there were only two pupils, and I was busy shaping my cup.

"This looks fascinating," she remarked and walked over to examine some of the pieces I had made at the art school, which were now displayed on the mantelpiece. "Can you teach me to make pretty things like this?"

"I'm sure you'll learn easily," said I . . . uneasily.

She peeled off her driving gloves. "Lend me an apron and I'll start at once."

I let her have one of my clean smocks and gave her a lump of clay that I had already wedged. I noticed the gems flashing on her hands as her fingers tentatively felt and squeezed the clay. I thought it would be interesting to learn to make jewelry and work with the pure colors of rubies and emeralds.

"This is the first day of my classes, and I haven't advertised," I explained. "I am giving nineteen lessons of three hours each, for fifteen dollars. I shall teach on five days a week, and my pupils will have a choice of morning or afternoon. If they feel like working all day, it will be thirty dollars."

Mrs. Bellair gave a gracious nod. "Very reasonable. I'll pay you in advance and take the morning class. If I find myself intrigued, I may take an afternoon course in weaving. I see you have two looms."

I showed Mrs. Bellair how to make pinch pots, which amused her. "I could make a tiny tea set for my granddaughter," she remarked. "My fingers are so small that I can easily pinch these miniature pots."

The girls had played with plasticine and modeling clay

when they were younger, and Lyn showed a good deal of skill. She was making a squirrel, watching one in a tree outside the window. Susan was having trouble with the legs of a horse.

"I shall have to teach you to make an armature," I told her, "and then you can make larger horses."

I made a note in my little book to buy wire for making armatures and plaster of Paris for casting. This venture of mine was beginning to loom into something larger. I should have to teach them to make templates, and that would mean buying materials and tools. However, there was no hurry for those. They could keep themselves busy with figurines, bowls, and jugs for some time to come.

"There," said Mrs. Bellair after a while, "there's a duck of a pinch pot. Will you bake it, and I can give it to little Joan?"

"I will as soon as I have enough pottery dry to be worthwhile heating the kiln," I promised.

The corners of her mouth went down. "I hope that will be very soon. I don't like to be kept waiting."

At twelve o'clock I told Lyn and Susan to wrap their figurines in damp cloths and put them in cans. Mrs. Bellair opened her handbag and took out a checkbook. "You will see me tomorrow," she said as she wrote a check. "I may be a little bit late. What is the penalty for tardiness?"

"Only that you have a shorter lesson," I said, and she laughed. She stood up and took off my smock. "I don't seem to have dirtied it, but if you like, I'll take it home and have my maid wash it." She wiped her hands on her handkerchief and put on her driving gloves.

"Oh, it's perfectly clean and hardly rumpled," I replied. "I'll hang it in the clothes closet till I need it."

I was relieved that Mrs. Bellair seemed so human, and the check gave me confidence. She said good-by and went out. The girls had produced paper bags of sandwiches.

"May we take our lunch out in the orchard?" Lyn asked. "Our mothers say we can take weaving lessons in the afternoon."

"We'll bring our money tomorrow," Susan said.

I was startled. I hadn't expected sudden success. "Sure," I answered. "You may wash your hands in the powder room. I'll get you some towels."

As I went for the towels, I was composing an advertisement to put in the local press. During the lunch hour I wrote one out and telephoned it to the advertising departments of two papers. I wondered if it would bring me results.

4

Pat Terry

As I washed my hands for lunch I was surprised to find that I was tired. It hadn't seemed strenuous at the time, but I could see that teaching and at the same time modeling a cup according to the drawing I had made had been more of a strain than I had realized. It was a good thing that I was eased into it gently, before my real troubles began.

At one I was back in the studio. I heard a car drive up, and in a minute the doorbell rang. I made a note to tell my pupils to come in without ringing or knocking to save me from trotting to the door when I was busy. Pat Terry was there, looking eager but nervous, while his mother waited in the car to make sure he was welcomed in. He had dragged himself up the three steps to the wide doorstep. As I opened the screen door I thought how pitifully thin and tired he looked.

"Come in, Pat," I said. "I'm so glad you're coming to my class. We're having fun. I do hope you'll get a kick out of it. After this, when you know the way to the studio, come in without ringing the bell. Do you think studio sounds too long-hair? Should we call it the workroom?"

I was chattering to cover his slow, dragging steps as I led him to the studio. "Do you want to do pottery or weaving this afternoon?"

Pat answered nervously, "A fellow I know, a veteran, learned to weave when he was in the hospital, and he makes a comfortable living. I thought I'd like to try my hand at it. If I could get orders, I could contribute to the family expenses instead of being a parasite."

"Splendid idea," I said absently. Good land, I was thinking, I've run into a snag. The girls have stayed to take a lesson in weaving and I have only two looms, and not a vast supply of thread. Talk about leaping without looking! I certainly had done that very thing. While I did some frantic thinking, I was stalling by showing Pat my craft pieces and giving a high-brow talk on design. His thin, pale face lighted up like a lamp.

Pat was so lean, almost emaciated, that his clothes hung loosely on him. His eyes were dark and pathetic. He was wearing a blue tartan sports shirt and gray flannel trousers.

"If I were you, I'd try different crafts," I said cagily. "You'll be bored to tears if you stick to weaving. Leather work pays well too, and you can have fun with clay." I gently steered him toward the table and showed him the cup I had been working on. "I have to put a handle on it," I remarked.

"I like that," Pat said. "It's an unusual shape."

"I'm going to put a design on it and glaze it," I went on,

hoping he would be intrigued, "and also on the sugar and cream that go with it, and I'm going to try selling to tourists."

"That's an idea," he said. "Do you suppose I could do that?"

I looked at his long nervous hands. "I don't see why you couldn't. Would you like to work a lump of clay and see how it feels? I'll wedge some for you."

The girls had come in and were waiting to be started on the looms. If there is one monotonous job on this green earth, it is tying the warp on a loom. I showed Lyn how to set up the big loom with cotton thread and Susan the cradle loom. I had to show her a number of times how to put the thread through the holes in the reed, or heddle, around the back roller and the front roller, and tie a weaver's knot.

"You must always remember to put a double thread at each selvage," I told her.

"You'll have to remind me," Susan said helplessly.

"Save your old nylon stockings to cut into strips for weaving the ends of a scarf, for the fringe," I explained. "You pull them out and it leaves the fringe, and then you stitch to make it firm."

"Gosh, I don't have any old nylons," Susan wailed.

"Ask your mother and your friends." I was trying hard to keep my patience with her.

I knew the tying would keep them busy for some time. I had some sheets of paper and crayons ready for them when they were tired of tying so that I could give them a lesson in design. If only Pat would get interested in clay, I could manage for a few days, but I must get another loom pronto. I was glad Mrs. Bellair had paid me in advance.

I heard an impatient sound from Pat Terry and went

quickly to help him. His black brows were drawn into a frown, and the corners of his mouth were fretful. I soon learned that I must cope with a semi-invalid who had been spoiled and pampered by his adoring mother.

"Having a little trouble, Pat?" I asked brightly. I could see darned well that he was.

"It goes all lop-sided," he complained. "When I try to round it on one side, it bulges on the other."

"I'll teach you the coil method. See, like this."

He enjoyed rolling his clay into a long pencil shape and coiling it around. "There's something rather intriguing about this," he said.

There was a shriek from Susan. "Penelope, what shall I do? I've got it all in a tangle."

As I straightened out the threads, I wondered if Susan would ever learn to model clay or weave thread. The poor child seemed to be equipped with ten thumbs. Was it honest to keep her on as a pupil and take her good money? Perhaps I might be able to turn some of the thumbs into fingers. Anyway, I was stuck with the job.

During the last hour of the lesson I let my pupils draw with crayons and taught them some of the principles of design.

"I used to get good marks for drawing and design at school," Pat Terry remarked. "I believe I might make a success of craft work, I really do." His dark eyes glowed, and his cheeks were flushed.

Just then I heard Mother calling me to answer the telephone. "Excuse me," I said. "Carry on with your drawing, and I'll be back in a minute."

I picked up the receiver of the old wall phone. "Penelope speaking."

"This is Doreen Hartley. I teach Grade I in Kelowna. I

heard about your craft class and I guess I could learn something that would help me in teaching the little tykes."

In a few minutes I had another pupil, as of tomorrow. I hurried back to my class of three. "We're going to have a school teacher studying with us, so we'll all have to be on our toes."

"Oh, gosh!" exclaimed Lyn.

"I hope it isn't one of my teachers," Susan said anxiously.

I laughed. "She teaches Grade I, so I don't think you need worry, but, being a teacher, she'll probably give us some competition."

"We may have competition, but you won't," Pat Terry gave me a boost. "Don't start hauling down your flag for anyone."

Pat was looking tired, and I knew he ought to rest, but I didn't want to suggest cutting his lesson short. "Don't push yourself too hard," I told him quietly. "Stop whenever you feel like taking a recess. I must find out what you all want to make, so I can order thread and leather and another loom. Lyn, what had you in mind to weave?"

"I'd like to make a tea cloth for my mother for Christmas."

"What colors would you like? Green with a white line makes a pretty effect."

"I'd like that," Lyn nodded. She was suggestible.

Susan had no idea. "How would you like to make a tray cloth, white and green?" I suggested.

"That would be OK."

Pat was grinning as he said, "I'd like to make a set of place mats, green and white check. There'd be enough green and white for that, wouldn't there?"

"You can have a wide choice of colors," I told him. "They'll all be used in the end."

"As you have to outlay for materials, I'd like to pay you in advance. That's the usual custom, isn't it?" He took out his wallet and handed me three fives.

The two girls looked at each other. "I'll bring my money tomorrow," Lyn said.

"I will too." Susan sounded doubtful.

"I'd like to own my loom," Pat said. "Will you order one of these small looms for me?"

I made a list of supplies and sent off an airmail letter with a money order to a store in Vancouver that stocks all sorts of craft needs. Until my order arrived, we should have to manage with what I had.

Promptly at nine the next morning Doreen Hartley arrived. She was twenty, she told me, and had been teaching for a year. Her eyes were bright and eager behind pixie spectacles with green rims studded with rhinestones. She would have been attractive if she had not been cursed with a sallow complexion and too much poundage.

"I just know I'm going to have a wonderful time and learn some lovely techniques," she chattered. "I took art at summer school at the university last year, and I simply loved it. Some of my little tads do such wonderful modeling with their modeling clay that I just can't keep ahead of them. I'd like to take weaving and design and glove making. Do you teach flower arranging?"

"I'm sorry, I've never studied flower arranging. I'd like to introduce Lyn Brown and Susan Smither. This is Miss Hartley, girls."

"Doreen, *please*," she cried. "I'm just a girl back in school and I'd like to forget the 'Miss Hartley' for a while. It always sounds so stiff."

Lyn had brought a check for the course, morning and afternoon. Susan had ten dollars on account, with a prom-

ise of the balance next day. Doreen quickly got the idea
and fished in her large handbag for her checkbook.

The three girls began working with clay. I set Doreen to
wedging a lump, hoping that would keep her quiet.

"I guess the air is all out of it now," she said after she
had thrown it down three times.

"We'll see." I laid the clay on the table and cut it in
half. "See the air holes. You aren't making Swiss cheese. If
you put a cup or vase in the kiln with air bubbles in it, they
expand with the heat and explode and wreck not only your
piece but other pottery being baked at the same time and
spoil other students' work and make you unpopular."

"Oh, mercy! That would be terrible. How many times do
I have to fling it on the floor?"

"Just until the air is all out."

After that she was quiet for a while. There was no noise
in the studio except the thump of clay on the canvas. I was
able to put the handle on my cup, after which I drew
and cut a template for a vase. I made that into a lecture
and demonstration, so that I was teaching while I worked.

Mrs. Bellair came in late. When I had introduced Doreen, I helped the older lady to turn a pinch pot into a
doll's jug. "I must make a set of doll's dishes for my
granddaughter," she said. "When I was a child, I used to
make cups and saucers of clay and put them in the oven to
bake, but they always fell to pieces and I was *so* discouraged."

"How frustrating!" Doreen squealed. "I used to make
tea sets out of those large poppy-seed pods, but they soon
faded."

At lunch Dad gave me a quizzical smile. "How is the
arts and crafts school coming along?"

"I have five pupils, three of them full time, and they

seem to like the work." I was cautious about boasting.
"They haven't actually finished any pieces yet. They're just
getting the feel of the clay."

"Have they paid you in advance?" Dad asked. "I understand this venture is a money-making concern, not just to
give pleasure to your pupils."

"Four of them have paid for the course, and one has
given me an advance and a promise."

"That's not too bad." He sounded relieved. "I hope
you'll be able to float your own ship, because I'm incon-
veniently short just now. In fact, there's a man I ought to
let out, for laziness and insolence, but I can't fire him because I can't pay him."

"Oh, Dad!" I cried. "I'm doing this to help the family.
How much do you owe the man?"

"Only forty dollars, but forty dollars looks like four hundred to me at this moment."

"I can let you have it this very minute. I have it in the
pocket of my smock." I jumped up and pushed the bills
into his pocket.

"This is only a loan, remember," Dad said. "I'm hoping
you will be able to finish your training and get your diploma. I'll talk to the bank manager tomorrow."

I kissed his bald spot. "Don't you worry, Dad. I'll make
the grade, and I'm learning while I teach."

"Teaching is the best way to learn anything," Mother
commented.

That evening I saddled Goldie and went for a long ride,
often stopping to look around and enjoy the beauty of the
sunset. I rode across the bridge and up to the Belgo lands,
then northward until the crimson of the sunset grew pale
and faded away entirely, leaving a sky clear as glass with

pricks of light showing as the first stars came out. I rode home slowly, feeling a delicious sort of tiredness. Goldie needed the exercise badly. Although I had not ridden fast, his golden coat was darkened by sweat.

He needed grooming too. His lovely silver mane and tail had not felt the curry comb for weeks, for no one had time to groom him. Although it was late and I was tired, I turned on a light and found the curry comb and the dandy brush. I combed his mane and tail and took out the burrs and went over him with a cloth and the dandy brush.

I was just turning Goldie loose in the pasture when Eric came sauntering along. "That's a good-looking horse you have, Pen," he remarked. "He isn't much use to you when you're away at school most of the year. If you can't raise the funds for your last year in Vancouver, I should think you'd sell him. You should get a good price. He's a pedigreed horse and a prize jumper."

"Sell Goldie!" I yelped. "I'd as soon think of selling you."

"Well, thanks, pal," he muttered.

"And I wouldn't dream of selling you, even if a buyer offered a million dollars."

"Then you'd be nuts," he said calmly and strolled away, leaving me shattered.

If I had to choose between Goldie and a diploma, which would it be? Why did that teasing boy show me a way out that had never occurred to my one-track mind? Was Goldie a luxury I didn't rate? Were Dad and Mother wondering why I didn't do what seemed to Eric the obvious thing? I couldn't—I just *couldn't*—face the thought of parting with Goldie. I had bought him as a yearling, before I started studying art, and trained him myself. During vaca-

tions I had practiced for gymkhanas and entered for jumping contests, and I had won two silver cups. It would be
ungrateful to Goldie to sell him.

"I love that horse," I vowed to myself. "I'll only part with
him as a last resort. My craft school simply must be made
to pay."

5

Tony Lestrange

The very next day I received a curious letter:

Dear Miss Warburton,

Your advertisement intrigues me. I would like to take your course as I wish to become an expert potter. As I live too far from you to be a day scholar, I should like to come as a boarder, if your mother will permit me. A camp cot on the veranda would be ample accommodation, and I could bring my own sleeping bag. If I do not receive a telegram or telephone message to forbid me, I shall arrive the day after you receive this letter.

Yours hopefully,
Tony Lestrange.

"Mother, do read this letter and tell me what you think of it." I handed it to her. She read it with a puzzled expression on her face.

"He doesn't give us much time to decide whether we

want a boarder. If we don't arm to repel boarders, he'll be on our doorstep before we know it. I must consult Dad."

Dad was out in the orchard. Mother went to find him while I returned to my pupils. I was not sure that I was capable of teaching this brash young man to be an expert potter. At noon we were able to have a family consultation.

"I can't teach a man to be an expert potter, can I?" I doubted.

"I'm not sure that I want a young man as a boarder," Mother said, "especially one I don't know."

"I've heard of the Lestranges," Dad recollected. "They're considered high brow and slightly eccentric, but nothing to worry about. If this young man is content to camp on the veranda and take the full course, I think we should let him come. It looks as if it might be hard to stop him," he added with a smile.

All the rest of the day I wondered about Tony Lestrange. Was he young or middle-aged? Perhaps he was a whiskery old fellow smoking a pipe that smelled like rags burning. Suppose that he was an arrogant teen-ager. Did he have so much money that he didn't care how much the board cost? or did he never pay his bills anyway? I went to bed still wondering and a teeny bit scared.

One thing I was sure about, and that was that I couldn't afford to refuse a pupil without having a rock-bottom reason. I was happily working with my pottery class next morning when I heard a most appalling racket. I thought a jet plane had flown too low and was tearing up the driveway. I made a dive for the window. The noise stopped just as I looked out.

"Oh, no!" I whispered. "Oh, *no!*"

A Tatraplan, a remarkable car made in Czechoslovakia and phenomenally noisy when old, had stopped in front of the house, and a young man was getting out. He wore a sports shirt, gray flannel trousers, and a beret. There was nothing alarming about his appearance, but the sight that stopped my heart for a beat was a Great Dane that was stepping with dignity out of the back seat. He looked to me as large as a Shetland pony.

Mac will want to fight him, I thought. Mac will never accept an enormous dog like that as a guest. Even for a Great Dane the dog looked extra large—and he was a sort of elephant gray. I heard the doorbell ring, and I knew Mother was out in the vegetable garden.

"Excuse me a minute," I said to my class, and I went to open the front door.

"Miss Warburton?" asked the young man, taking off his beret. "My name is Tony Lestrange. I trust my letter reached you yesterday."

"Come in, Mr. Lestrange," I said. "We did get your letter, but you didn't mention your dog. I'm afraid our dog won't like him."

"He's very quiet. He never fights," Tony Lestrange said soothingly. "I couldn't mention him in my letter, because I didn't acquire him until this morning. I met a chap in Kelowna who was in a fix because he was offered a job for the summer but he couldn't take a dog, so he asked me to take care of him and he gave me a huge stock of dog biscuits and his bowl for water, so I couldn't refuse, could I?"

"There are kennels where you can board dogs," I said severely. "Will you come into the living room and sit down while I call my mother?"

I sprinted out to the garden where Mother was picking peas. "Mother, come quickly," I gasped. "This Tony Lestrange has come and brought another man's Great Dane with him, and he drives a Tatraplan, a terribly noisy car."

Poor Mother! I should have broken it more gently. "Heavenly day!" she said and stood there looking stricken, while green peas dropped out of her hand.

"Do come," I urged. "I must go back to my pupils."

With a deep sigh Mother followed me to the house and into the living room.

"Mother, this is Mr. Lestrange. I'll leave you to make the arrangements, because I must go back to my class. You know my terms."

When I went back to the studio, I found the class buzzing. Susan was gazing out the front window. "What an enormous dog," she said, turning to me, "and that's a Tatraplan. I know a boy that drives a Tatra."

A little later Mother brought Tony Lestrange to the studio. "Mr. Lestrange and I have agreed that if Mac objects to the Great Dane, he'll take him to a kennel."

"It will be a last resort," Tony Lestrange said. "A big dog like Hamlet needs plenty of exercise and room to rove. I hope you will call me Tony. 'Mr. Lestrange' makes me think I am my father."

He walked over to the table and looked with interest at the work going on. I introduced him to Mrs. Bellair and the girls. Mrs. Bellair looked at him with gimlet eyes and said sharply, "I'm surprised at a young man like you wanting to model in clay."

Tony gave the lady a look of swift dislike. "A deposit of pottery clay has been discovered on my father's estate, and, as his fruit isn't paying very well, he wants to start a small pottery plant. I am to learn the trade and teach my brothers and sisters. I trust the explanation satisfies you."

His tone was very soft, very silky, and very dangerous. This is what people in New Zealand call earthquake weather, I thought. I bet there'll be trouble between these two all the time, and I don't know how to prevent it. Somehow I'd have to keep the peace.

"You would like to start work," I said to Tony. "There's room at this end of the table."

I took him to the end of the long table farthest from Mrs. Bellair. "I'll show you how to wedge clay to drive out the air bubbles."

I kept on talking while I demonstrated, because I could see Mrs. Bellair sending sharp glances at Tony, and I knew she was ready to throw another dart at him. If I didn't keep them from fighting, I might lose one pupil, or both. Even if they got a kick out of a private war, the rest of us would prefer peace.

"Yes, I see," Tony said. "I want to understand the whole theory behind the practice, so I can teach it intelligently. I shall probably be foreman when my father starts his factory, and I must know the why as well as the way."

He sounds sensible, I thought, even if he did pick up a Great Dane to bring along. Perhaps he's just one of those people who are crazy about dogs. His rather puckish face was sober and intent as he rolled the clay into long cylinders for building in coils. His thin, dark features suggested French ancestry, and his gray-green eyes were often lighted with a spark of deviltry.

At the noon break Mrs. Bellair went home, which eased the strain. I showed Tony his room, and he carried his suitcase, sleeping bag, and a violin case up the stairs.

"I hope you won't mind if I practice my violin sometimes. I warn you I'm no Yehudi Menuhin."

Later we found out that this was a triumph of understatement. I think there is no sound that can put a knife through your brain like a violin played out of tune.

Dad came in from the cherry orchard with Mac at his

heels. We watched with misgivings while Mac walked stiff-
legged around the Great Dane, rumbling in his throat.
Hamlet might have been deaf and blind for all the attention he paid. After a while Mac seemed awed by the big
dog's indifference and decided to make friends. They went
gamboling off together.

"I told you Hamlet wouldn't fight," Tony Lestrange reminded us. "Great Danes are usually peaceable, though little dogs yap at them in a frenzy of terror."

Meanwhile, Dad was sizing up the young man. I had
said, as I introduced him, "Tony's father has a deposit of
pottery clay on his ranch and he is planning a small factory, so Tony is learning to make pottery, to be the foreman." I was sure Dad would have doubts about a man who
was physically fit wanting to make pottery as a hobby.

"Very interesting. Hope you'll make a go of it, Lestrange," he said quite cordially, and we all went in to lunch.

Tony set to work to charm and amuse. He told stories
that had us all in stitches, especially Eric. The lunch hour
whistled by. As I was clearing the table, my young brother
said to me, "What a man! You'd better keep him, Pen."

"Ha!" I replied, "I'd as soon carry firecrackers in my
pocket. You never know when he'll explode."

The afternoon passed quietly, except for Doreen's chattering over her work. She kept up a running commentary.
"Oh, how silly of me! This clay is too dry. When will I
learn to make an even roll? Even a child in my class could
do better than this. I know you'll give me a bad mark,
Penelope. I'll never earn a star."

Once or twice Tony Lestrange looked up from his work
with an amused smile at the yaketty-yak, but he didn't
make the crack I dreaded. The young girls gave occasional
squeaks of dismay over their weaving. Pat and Tony con-

centrated on their work, and I was able to try an experiment with mine.

You may remember my mentioning the red clay that bakes to a rich brown. I took my cup that was still damp and with a stylus drew the form of an Ogopogo I had designed. Then I applied red clay to the design in raised relief. I hoped it would be effective when I baked the piece and gave it a pale-green glaze. At four o'clock my pupils went home, but I went on working.

"Do you mind if I stick around and practice?" Tony asked. "I won't so much as speak to you, and you can forget I'm here."

"OK," I said. So, for an hour we worked in complete silence, and I was falling in love with my design. I should have to vary it a little to curl around the saucer. I had intended to paint the Ogopogo on, but this seemed to me more original, and it would save a second baking. Since my kiln was small and I would have my pupils' work to bake, this was a consideration.

At five I left Tony to carry on as he liked, and I quickly put on my jodhpurs and went for a short gallop on Goldie. It refreshed me after the long day in the studio, and it was exercise my horse needed.

"Goldie, it would hurt me terribly to have to sell you, but I guess I won't have to. It looks as if I shall be able to make enough money for my fourth year, especially if I baby-sit for my board in Vancouver."

His paces were so easy that I wasn't the least bit stiff or sore after a ride, even though my muscles had been growing soft at loom and easel. His mouth was tender, and I hardly had to use the reins, for he was trained to obey hand signals. What a horse! as Eric would say.

At dinner that evening Mother remarked to Tony, "The

Great Dane seems content to wander around the orchard. You aren't afraid he'll run away and go back to Kelowna, are you?"

"I certainly hope he won't," Tony said airily, "because he's a pedigreed dog, and I happen to know that his owner refused a thousand dollars for him."

"Rather a responsibility for you," Dad commented. "What will you do if he gets lost or stolen?"

"One has to take chances," Tony replied calmly. "His owner won't hold me responsible, provided that I give him as good care as I can."

I was thinking how dreadful it would be if Mac ever sank those sharp teeth in Hamlet's throat and closed that long collie jaw on it. Hamlet was twice the size and weight of Mac but probably had only half the fighting technique.

"Yes, I suppose he's a responsibility," Tony frowned as if it were a new idea to him, "but think how miserable the poor animal would have been shut up in a boarding kennel. Oh, he'll do famously."

I must admit that Tony fed the dog regularly and kept his bowl filled with water. Hamlet slept on Tony's sleeping bag, for Mother had supplied my pupil with proper bedding.

Mother and the foreman's wife had been busy all day, canning cherries. Mother was tired out and went to lie down in the living room while Eric and I cleared away and washed the dishes. Suddenly she leaped from the couch with a cry of fright. "What on earth is that?"

A sound like dragging rusty nails out of a wall came from upstairs, accompanied by a mournful howl of the depth and volume of a church bell, but not so musical. Eric and I listened, with dishes drying in our hands, until we could make out the tune of "Home on the Range."

"Suffering cats!" cried Eric. "What is it?"

"Hamlet meeting his father's ghost," I giggled. "I saw Tony carrying in a violin case, and he said he hoped we didn't mind if he practiced."

"That's no violin," Eric retorted. "I've heard a violin. It didn't sound like that at all."

"He said he was no Yehudi Menuhin, and Hamlet seems to take it hard."

Mother came out to the kitchen. "This is more than even I can stand. Penelope, he's your problem. Go up and beg him to stop on Hamlet's account."

I went up and tapped on Tony's door, which stood open. The noises stopped.

"I know what you're going to say," my pupil predicted. "You're going to put in a plea for a dumb animal whose feelings are being lacerated, if you can call Hamlet dumb."

"Some dogs are terribly affected by music," said I, the little diplomat.

"Yes, you're so right," Tony agreed sadly. "I can see that while I have Hamlet with me I'll have to refrain from playing my fiddle." He chuckled. "That old refrain, you know. I shall get painfully out of practice. Did you ever hear a dog with a more resounding voice?"

"I certainly never did," I answered with conviction.

As I turned to go downstairs, I saw him reluctantly putting his violin in its case. You never can tell, I thought. I had been really scared of trouble when I saw Hamlet get out of the car, and now it turned out that he was saving us from evenings of agony. We'll have to find Tony some books to keep him entertained. Too bad we don't have TV, but probably Hamlet would howl at that.

I went back to the studio to make a saucer with the Ogopogo design in red clay though I would much have preferred to lounge with a magazine on the veranda in the pleasant evening air. I knew that I must work long hours and keep going fast. The fear of having to sell Goldie was a continual incentive. I must ride my hobby hard if I wanted to continue riding my horse.

I drew a design for a teapot, with the Ogopogo head for a spout. I would make a teapot, cream and sugar, and six cups and saucers. When they were glazed, I would take them to Kelowna to Esselmont's China Store. Mr. Esselmont sells gifts as well as china, and the tourists go there for souvenirs. His son Garth helps him in the store. Garth was in Grade XII when I was in X, and twice he came to our Christmas dances. I thought he was a dreamboat, but far beyond my reach. I was pretty sure that Mr. Esselmont would be willing to sell my wares on commission, even though he might not risk buying them outright. I was dreaming happily when Tony came into the studio and stood with his hands in his pockets, staring at me gloomily.

"You are indefatigable," he said. "I should get bored to tears if I kept on at this job hour after hour. I am feeling annoyed with Hamlet for making such an uproar about my fiddling. I could have put in two good hours of practice if it hadn't been for his making such a row. After all, it was a bit of cheek for a chap I hardly knew to unload his dog on me, wasn't it?"

"I guess he thought you had a tongue," I said, silently thanking Hamlet.

"What does one do in a place like this?" he asked. "I can't drive into Kelowna every evening to go to a show or have a swim."

"If you wait till I finish this drawing, I'll take you out to the pasture and show you my golden horse," I offered.

"Wonderful," he said. "I love horses. I ride rather well, you know."

Ten minutes later we went out into the cool, golden evening to see my golden horse. "By cracky! He *is* a beauty!" Tony exclaimed. "Part Arab I should say, judging by his lines and the shape of his head. I do consider myself a judge of horses. Perhaps you'll let me ride him sometimes?"

"Hm. Not many people get a chance to ride Goldie," I said, "because I've trained him to obey hand signals, and ordinary bridle riding would confuse him."

"That's OK. I can use hand signals," replied my brash new pupil.

6

The Picnic

When I whistled, Goldie came trotting to the pasture bars and lowered his fine head to take an apple from my hand with his velvety lips. Tony patted his neck.

"Just as I said—he's part Arab, the faithful steed of the stories. And what a pace! He doesn't trot. He flows. I certainly would love to ride him."

"Some day I may feel generous," I said cautiously. "As I just told you, I don't let everyone ride Goldie. I like to know that a rider can use hand signals and is easy on a horse's mouth and won't ride him into a lather or let him stumble."

"You can trust me," Tony declared. "I have a row of medals for jumping."

"That's fine," I said, but I was thinking how well pleased he seemed to be with his violin playing, and I was scared he might not be any more a horseman than he was a musician.

The days went on, and I was able to bake some of my pieces, and then a collection of my pupils' pottery. Thank goodness they all came out whole.

Mrs. Bellair and Tony kept needling each other. She made some unkind comment about every piece of pottery he made, and he answered her with caustic wit. They kept me in a state of jitters for fear the sparks would start a real blaze.

That summer was almost cloudless, with the hot sun blazing down day after day, but even so the lighting in the studio was not so good as it should be for art work. Our house faced north, and the studio took up the whole side of the western wall. The veranda shaded the living room and kitchen, with doors into it from both, so that it was easy to serve meals on the veranda, which was sunny and pleasant in the early morning and cool in the evening. The studio was shaded from the late sun by a row of Lombardy poplars.

There are two side windows in the studio and one at the end, but their light was dulled by these heavy poplars, so that sometimes we had to use artificial light. As there was only one outlet apart from the chandelier, this was not always enough.

"The light is worse than usual this morning," Mrs. Bellair fretted one day. "I really cannot see what I'm doing. You have a good light where you are, Mr. Lestrange. You can easily see your vase . . . I presume it *is* a vase—it doesn't look like anything else recognizable."

"What a good thing that I can see my vase, which is a joy to behold!" Tony responded cheerfully. He gave a quick glance at the figurine Mrs. Bellair was modeling. "How fortunate for you the light there is not so good!"

Doreen sputtered with laughter and turned it into a

cough. Mrs. Bellair glared at each in turn. I tried to ignore the whole battle, for I felt too young and inexperienced to control a woman three times my age, and a man older than myself, who had a dagger for a tongue.

"I'll turn on the electric light, Mrs. Bellair," I said, and pressed the switch button.

Tony muttered, "Perhaps a candle . . . or a rush-light . . ."

I gave him a lethal look, but he didn't see it.

Tony sat and watched Mrs. Bellair's fingers, with the gems flashing on them, and suddenly exclaimed, "I bet I could make a figurine. It doesn't look too hard. Tomorrow I'll make a little dog, a little snappy dog."

"Why snappy?" I asked. I didn't like the mischief in his eyes and the little smile at the corners of his mouth. That slight smile was a danger signal.

Next morning, sure enough, he was absorbed in modeling a dog sitting up and begging. That same smile was playing around his mouth, and I felt uneasy, though I couldn't see any harm in his making a dog.

"Why don't you make a figurine of Hamlet?" I asked. "He's such a handsome dog!"

"I'm not clever enough to model all those fine muscles," he explained in what sounded like a reasonable answer. "With this little dog I can hide my errors in anatomy with curly hair, but a Dane is so stark."

When the dog was completed, I saw Tony take an envelope out of his pocket and put something on the paws. I caught a glint of brightness and went behind him to see over his shoulder. Lyn was curious too and came to peer over his other shoulder.

Tony picked the dog up and turned it to face us. Lyn gave a smothered squeak. "Why, it's got a face like . . ."

I had my hand over her mouth then and squeezed her arm to silence her. The little snappy dog had a face that was a portrait of Mrs. Bellair, and the paws, held up to beg, were decorated with minute specks of glass that twinkled like the diamonds in the lady's rings.

For a moment I was petrified. Then I wheeled my big guns into action. I gave Lyn a look that sent her back to her work, and I took the dog from Tony's hand. "This is too easily spoilt to be left around. I'll put it in a can in a safe place."

I always took great care of the unbaked pieces, so no one paid any attention to that remark. I silently fumed until twelve o'clock, when Mrs. Bellair went home. As soon as I could get him alone, I turned my wrath loose on Tony.

"You will please blot off that face and those specks of glass," I said, "and never insult one of my pupils again."

He opened his eyes so wide they almost dropped out. "Face?" he queried in a blank tone. "Glass? My dear young lady, what are you talking about?"

"You know quite well," I answered hotly. "You made the dog's face a portrait, a very clever portrait, I'll admit, of Mrs. Bellair."

"What a preposterous suggestion!" he exclaimed. "It would take a woman to think of such an idea. If there is a remote likeness, it must have been due to my subconscious. I wouldn't insult a dog by making it look like that lady."

"Did your subconscious prompt you to put diamonds on the dog's paws?" I demanded.

I was so mad I could have gone up in smoke.

"Preposterous!" he said again. "I have no diamonds. Let me see my dog and remove any trace of likeness that may have accidentally crept into the clay. You must be imagining things. I suppose you have a vivid imagination."

I brought the can and took off the lid. Flames were still spouting out of my eyes, mouth, and nose. I lifted out the dog and set it on the table. It looked so like Mrs. Bellair making a complaint while her hands held the clay that I could hardly keep from laughing.

With a quick flick of his finger Tony wiped off the face. "What are you talking about?" he asked in an aggrieved tone of voice. "I don't see even a dog's face. It isn't finished yet."

"That doesn't account for the diamonds on the paws," I argued, "even though you have removed the other evidence."

His expression grew more impish than ever. "Now, look here, if you nag me much more, I'll put *your* portrait on the face and see how you like that."

What could you do with such a man? I burst into tears.

"Bless my soul! My dear girl, I was only joking. I wouldn't dream of putting your portrait on the little beast. Look." He carefully picked out the specks of glass and then squeezed the dog in his hands until it was once more a lump of clay.

I pulled my handkerchief out of my smock pocket and mopped up my face. "That isn't what made me cry. I've been enduring the strain of you and Mrs. Bellair feuding until this was the last straw. I just wish I'd never started a class. I could have worked peacefully by myself making pottery."

"You must admit I never start it," Tony pleaded. "Every time there's been a battle, the old battle ax has drawn first blood."

"I know you don't start it," I agreed, "but your wit is too devastating, and you shouldn't use it on a weak woman, even if she is annoying."

"Why don't you bawl her out for everlastingly picking on me?"

I giggled. "I will," I promised, "the very first time she makes a figurine of an animal with your face on it."

He gave a shout of laughter. "You win. I'll try to ignore Mrs. Bellair when she jabs at me and pretend I'm too much absorbed in my work to hear her."

"That will probably annoy her more than if you fight back," I agreed. "I should think she'd know by this time that she always gets the worst of it."

Mother called us to lunch then, and we went to wash our hands. Tony was slightly subdued when he came to the table and extra polite to Mother, Dad, and me.

When work started in the afternoon, Tony was at a small table in the corner, weaving a tartan scarf on a cradle loom, Lyn was weaving a fabric for a skirt on the large loom, Doreen was cutting a template, and Susan was drawing designs. Lyn had a talent and liking for crafts, but Susan only came to be with Lyn—she detested weaving and didn't like pottery. Pat was hooking a rug.

Craft experts sometimes claim handicrafts as a sure cure for all mental illness, but I am not so sure about that. I believe using the hands is good for the brain and the nerves, but it is no use forcing handwork on people like Susan, who just don't like crafts. It reminds me of the musician in a famous orchestra who burst into tears and sobbed, "But, Mr. Toscanini, I just don't like music."

Pat Terry was really getting a lot of good from my course. He looked happier and healthier already. Companionship meant a great deal to him, and he was sure he was on the way to making a living. He was a natural, and I was sure he would succeed.

"Even if I can't sell my stuff right away, I can help out at home," he told me. "I can make Christmas presents. I'll weave a skirt length for my mother and make place mats to save her buying a new tablecloth. Our hearthrug is badly burned. I'll hook a rug out of strips of worn-out sweaters."

He looked so happy and full of hope that I felt my course would have been worth the trouble just for that one pupil.

"By the time you have the house fixed up and your mother wearing hand-woven clothes, you'll have had enough practice to turn out marketable articles," I said. "You'll be able to take orders for place mats and all sorts of things. You mustn't work too hard and make yourself sick, though."

"I'm feeling better than I have for years," he replied.

"Why don't we have some fun for a change?" Susan asked. "Why don't we go down to the lake for a swim after school and buy hamburgers and have a picnic? Hamburgers and ice-cream will be enough, so we don't have to bother making sandwiches."

"I know why they call those revolving sandwich plates 'Lazy Susans,'" I laughed.

Susan laughed good-naturedly. She didn't even mind being called lazy.

"Susan's brain isn't lazy," Tony said, looking up alertly. "She's dreamed up a good plan. I have room for four or five in my Tatra."

"I can take four in my car," Doreen offered.

"Would you feel like going to a picnic?" I asked Pat.

"Oh, I would," he said and his eyes lighted up, "but my mother . . ."

"I'll call her on the phone," I said. "But what about swim suits?"

"I'll buzz home for mine," Susan said.

"I will too," Lyn chimed in. "You can let us out ten minutes early," she coaxed.

Since both girls came on bicycles, they would not take long to ride home for swim suits and towels.

"I have mine in my room," said Tony.

"I have two suits. I can lend you one and a towel," I told Doreen, "so we're all set."

I telephoned to Pat's mother and invited her to join us.

"Pat going to a picnic?" She sounded thrilled. "That will be lovely for him. I'll run over with his trunks and a towel, but I won't come, thank you, dear, because Pat will feel so independent without me."

Understanding mother, I thought.

I knew that Eric was making orchard boxes for the apple crop, so I went to the back door. "Hi, Eric," I shouted, "we're all going to the lake for a swim and a picnic. Want to come?"

"OK," he yelled back. "Do you know where my swimming trunks are?"

"I'll find them. You go and tell Mother we'll be out for dinner. She's in the vegetable garden."

In ten minutes we were ready to start. Doreen took Pat Terry, Lyn, and Eric in her nice safe car, and Susan and I got into the Tatraplan. It's an odd-looking car, with a spine sticking up over the back of it, and the engine in the rear.

"My Tatra isn't this year's model," Tony apologized. "In fact it's pretty old, and you may find it a trifle noisy."

He started the engine, and the thing let out a roar like a whole jungle full of angry lions. When it had shaken the house with its noise, it leaped into life and hurtled down the road. Tony was a reckless driver. He swung into the main road without stopping and swerved past an old Ford

driven by an elderly couple. I caught a glimpse of the
driver's shocked face as we passed within inches of him.
When we reached Kelowna, we stopped in a parking lot
with a jolt that nearly threw me through the windshield.

Some minutes later Doreen's car drew up beside us, and
we all went to the Aquatic Club to change into swim suits.
We were all members except Tony and we took him as a
guest. The summer had been so hot that the water was
beautifully warm and clear as glass. In the late afternoon
it was calm. We were all fairly good swimmers, so we dived
in. I was anxious about Pat, because he can swim only with
his arms and one leg, and even those limbs don't seem
strong. He saw my motherly look and smiled.

"It's OK, Penelope. I'll just putter around near the
shore."

The others had all swum out into the lake, so I followed
them. It felt delightful. The warm, clear water was not so
bracing as the salt sea I was used to, but it was cleaner. The
coolness after the hot day washed my tiredness away, yet
it was warm enough to invite a swimmer to stay in for a
long time. I swam far out and floated on my back to rest.
Then I trod water and looked around for the others.

I was beginning to swim back to shore, slowly, restfully,
when I heard a shout. "Help! Help!"

Pat! I started a fast crawl shoreward. Could I possibly
get there in time? Why had I been so far out? Would someone on shore go to the rescue? The lifeguard would surely
rescue Pat—if it was Pat.

By the time I was able to put my feet on the sand and
wade ashore, two swimmers had been rescued. Pat was lying on the beach, with the lifeguard and another man
bending over him. Others were around someone else—a
child.

"Is he all right?" I panted as I ran toward Pat.

The lifeguard turned his head. "He's OK. He tried to rescue a kid who'd caught a cramp."

Pat smiled up at me. "I'm fine, Penelope. Just a bit winded."

His face was a pale green that frightened me. "I have a vacuum bottle of hot tea in the car," I said. "Would you like a cup to warm you?"

"I sure would. I feel cold."

I ran as fast as I could to the parking lot and brought back the vacuum bottle. Pat was sitting up by that time, and he drank the hot tea gratefully.

"That's the stuff. It hits the spot."

"Shouldn't we take Pat to the hospital and let a doc give him the once-over?" asked the man who had been with the lifeguard. I saw then that he was dressed in a shirt and trousers and that they were wringing wet. I heard later that while the lifeguard had been bringing in the boy with the cramp, the other man had rescued Pat.

"Don't you remember me, Penelope?" he asked.

I looked up and saw his face then. "Of course, I remember you, Garth Esselmont," I replied.

Remember him? I should say I did. He was the handsomest boy in the high school, but he never dated a girl, because he had to work after school, helping his father in the china store, and he was saving to go to the university in Vancouver.

I had heard that he was at the university while I was at the School of Art, but we hadn't met. I did think he might have called me up or asked me for a date. But I reminded myself that among nine thousand university students there must be hundreds of pretty girls. Anyway, the university is miles from the art school in downtown Vancouver.

7

Garth Esselmont

"Garth pulled me ashore or I shouldn't have made it," Pat told me. "I'm OK. All I needed was a hot drink to buck me up. Is there any more tea in your vacuum bottle, Penelope?"

I filled his cup, and he drank it, clear and hot. "Don't take me to the hospital," he begged. "They'll phone my mother, and she'll get in a tizzy. I'll have a rubdown and get into my clothes and be ready for a hamburger."

I was sure his mother would get in a tizzy, and I should get the blame. Pat's color was coming back, and I thought he would be all right.

"We're going to buy hamburgers and ice-cream bars and have a picnic in the park. Will you come with us?" I invited Garth.

"As my guest," Pat added.

"I'll be glad to," Garth accepted. "Will there be time for me to have a short swim?"

"Of course. There isn't any deadline."

Garth and the lifeguard helped Pat to his feet, and Garth went with him to the Aquatic Club. In a short time they came out again, Pat dressed and looking his usual rather haggard self. Garth was in his swim trunks. They were a contrast, because Garth is tall, with a crew cut, and fairly radiates health. To me he looks handsome, but I am not sure whether other people would call him so. He hasn't much tan because he works such long hours in his father's store.

When Garth came in from his swim, we pooled our money, and Tony went off with the two young girls to buy hamburgers and ice-cream bars. The sun was still high and hot, so we found a shady place under the trees. Tony had bought ginger ale for all hands. "My treat," he said.

Garth sat down beside me. "I heard a buzz that you're teaching crafts out at The Poplars. Is that so?"

Here was my chance, handed to me with a hamburger. I hate to mix business with pleasure, but this opportunity was too good to pass up. I waved my hand at the group.

"This is my class. The girls were tired of weaving and asked for a little fun for a change. Personally I think crafts *are* fun."

"This is intriguing," Garth declared. "Where do you teach, and what?"

"You remember that large room where we danced at New Year?"

"I sure do. I missed it last year because I was on the coast."

"That's now my studio. I have an old ping-pong table and a smaller table for pottery and leather work, a big loom and several cradle looms. My kiln is in the basement."

Garth bit into a hamburger and didn't speak for a minute. He was looking thoughtful. "Your pupils aren't doing commercial work yet?" he supposed.

"Hardly yet, but I am." I came straight to the point. "I'm making a tea set with a raised brown Ogopogo under pale green glaze. I hope it will be attractive."

He grinned, but he seemed interested. "Tourist bait," he teased. "I'd like to see it. We sell plenty of tourist bait. Mind if I take a run out and see your class at work? And especially your own pottery?"

"We'd feel highly honored. We haven't had a visitor yet. I have a morning pupil who isn't here this evening—Mrs. Bellair."

A curious smile passed over Garth's face. "Mrs. Bellair is one of my dad's customers. She's kind of particular in her buying."

"I imagine she would be."

Garth was gazing out at the lake, watching a man on water skis towed by a fast motorboat. "That's my favorite sport," he remarked, "but this year I've been too busy to get out often. Have you tried it? It's grand sport."

"Diving is mine," I said, "and skiing in winter. One of the girls at the art school has a car, and we used to go up Seymour Mountain."

"I go up Grouse. That's why I've never bumped into you, I guess. Have you ever tried Hollyburn?"

"No. I'm only a beginner. I stay on the meadows on Seymour."

I had my eye on Pat, for he was sagging, though he was trying to act as if the near drowning hadn't hurt him, so I broke up the party early. Lyn and Susan wailed, "Why, we've just come."

"And now we're just going home," I said gaily. I didn't

want to say it was on Pat's account, or he would be embarrassed.

He said it for himself. "Don't break up the party on my account."

I made up an excuse. "We came away in such a hurry I left things I had to do. Sorry, kids, that's the way it is today. Some day we'll take time out for a longer picnic."

Doreen drove Pat Terry and the two girls to their homes, before she went to her own home in Kelowna, which was darned decent of her. Eric and I went with Tony in the Tatra. Eric was so fascinated by the foreign car that he wanted one for himself. It might have been all Tony claimed for it with a sane driver at the wheel. I was so thankful to reach home all in one piece that I made a silent vow never to get in the strange car again.

I had my tea set ready, pale green with the dark-brown Ogopogo coiled around each piece, when Garth arrived without warning to see my studio and my pottery.

"You sure have a good show here," he observed, looking around the studio. "Professional."

He was right. It did look professional, with Pat and Susan working at the looms, Tony smoothing off a jug, and Lyn sitting in front of the fireplace putting glaze on a bowl. We used the open chimney to carry off the fumes of the glaze. My tea set stood on a shelf.

Garth stood for ten minutes examining every piece of the tea set, inside and out. "I see you've signed them. Have you signed every piece?"

"Yes, every single piece." I was crazy to hear how he liked them.

"Is this set for sale?" he asked.

"Oh, yes, and I had some idea of starting a product,

Ogopogo pottery, for sale to tourists. What do you think about it?"

"I like it. Do you mind if I take one piece to show my father?"

"You're welcome," I said. My hopes were rising.

"Have you set a price on this set?"

"No, I haven't. I'd be glad of advice."

"If Dad buys it to sell, he'll count on making a good profit—I guess you know that—double what he pays you. There's a heavy risk in tourist trade."

I was startled to hear how much profit Mr. Esselmont would need, and I made up my mind to find some way of selling my wares to avoid a middleman, but for a start I'd be glad enough to accept whatever he considered a fair price, for I knew he was dependable.

"I'll leave it to your father, Garth," I agreed.

I found a box and soft paper for wrapping the cup and saucer safely and gave them to him.

"You were so wise to sign every piece," Garth said. "I expect Dad can put a good price on an original which is at present unique. I personally admire the design very much. I'll ask my dad to phone and let you know."

After that he looked at the work my pupils were doing. He was interested in the commercial end of all this work. "I guess you'll be wanting to keep your first attempts," he said, "but if you go on working, we'll be a market for your stuff."

Pat's eyes were dark, and I could see the thoughts going around in his head. This was going to be a great incentive for him. I was afraid that he'd overdo in his six weeks' plan to get his work on a paying basis.

After Garth had gone, Pat said to me, "Do you s'pose I

could take a morning course as well as the afternoon one, Penelope?"

"Will it suit your mother to bring you so early?" I asked a question instead of answering his.

"It won't make any difference to Mother, and I'm feeling fine. I can take it, if that's what's on your mind."

He certainly was in far better health than when he first came, and he was not fretful and demanding as he had been.

"I doubt if Esselmont's will be a market for my dad's factory wares," Tony observed. "Dad hasn't the giftie shoppe in mind. Our stuff will be cheap assembly-line crockery."

Late that afternoon Mr. Esselmont phoned me. "Garth has shown me the cup and saucer of your tea set, and he tells me every piece is flawless. That's very nice. Would you consider fifteen dollars a fair price? I can't ask more than twenty-five, and it's a risk."

"Whatever you say is right, Mr. Esselmont."

"Can you ship it in to me?"

"I'll bring it in tomorrow, early."

I knew Dad would let me have the car about eight in the morning, so I could run into town and be back in plenty of time for my class.

After I had talked to Mr. Esselmont, I did some figuring. Fifteen dollars would not pay good wages for the time I had taken to design, model, and bake the tea set. I knew I must find a quicker way of doing the work or be content with small pay. If I could sell my pottery directly to a customer, I'd do much better. In the meantime this was a chance to introduce my Ogopogo ware, and I was grateful to make a first sale so quickly.

I told my class in the morning, "We've made our first

sale. Mr. Esselmont has bought my tea set. I delivered it
to his store this morning."

Pat rubbed his thin hands. "We're on our way. I'd like to
design a vase with balsamroot sunflowers on it, yellow on
a gray background. Do you imagine Esselmont would buy
it?"

"It sounds attractive," I said. "Go to it, my lad."

"I don't want to sell my pieces," Doreen demurred. "I
want to make things for my own room and for presents.
So many of my friends are getting married these days, I'm
always buying presents."

"Me, too," said Lyn. "I'm going to make Christmas presents. My uncles are going to get ashtrays. It's too bad they
don't smoke."

"I don't think I'll ever make anything good enough to
sell," Susan said placidly.

"We need a potter's wheel," I declared. "The trouble
with having a wheel is that everyone wants it at once."

"You might find one in a second-hand store in a city,"
Tony suggested. "I can give you a list of addresses of second-hand and antique shops that have odd things like
that."

"We can make things without a wheel, surely," Doreen
disagreed. "I'd prefer to make vases and figurines the way
we have been doing. You can have your old potter's
wheel."

"You'd sing a different song if you'd ever used one," I
laughed.

"The bother about trying to make money out of crafts is
that you need so much equipment," I grumbled to Tony,
"and as you go on with it, you have to spend more and
more."

"My dad realizes that," Tony answered with a wry smile.

"He intends to make a capital outlay and use mass-production methods. The stuff won't be artistic, probably, unless I learn enough from you to be able to design beautiful shapes for mass production."

"I don't see why not," I said. "Peasant pottery is very pleasing. A good deal depends on the shapes and on the glazes you use."

Mother and I drove into town in the late afternoon to do a bit of shopping before the stores closed. I saw my tea set displayed in the center of Esselmont's store window. It was on a large tray, with a tall vase of flowers behind it, which made my pottery look extra attractive. I pointed it out to my mother.

"I'm sure someone will buy it," she said. "Even if no one does buy it, Mr. Esselmont will have a window display that will catch the eye of window shoppers and lure them into the store."

I dawdled, hoping to overhear some admiring comments and, sure enough, I did. An elderly lady caught her husband's arm and said, "Norman, do look at that tea set. It's really an original hand-made. Wouldn't it do nicely as a wedding present for Joan?"

"Ogopogo ware, eh?" I watched the husband's face to see if he would agree to buy it. I half wanted him to, and I half wanted to leave it there so that hundreds of people would see and talk about the new Ogopogo ware, every piece signed by the potter.

"I'll bet it costs a mint," he growled. "After all, Joan isn't even a relative."

"Well, come in and ask the price," his wife insisted, pulling his sleeve.

"My dear girl, we're late as it is, and if I let you loose in a china store, we'll never get home tonight."

"Like the old woman and the pig," his wife retorted with spirit. "Well, I know who's the pig."

I nearly burst out laughing. I would have waited for more shoppers to make comments, but Mother had gone ahead and was looking back for me, so I ran after her.

"You don't want to be arrested for loitering, do you?" she asked, shaking her head at me and smiling.

I laughed, for the tall handsome Royal Canadian Mounted Police constable often stops in at The Poplars for a glass of juice or a handful of cherries.

Mother and I were being stopped by friends every few yards. Mother was not above doing a public-relations job. "Have you seen Penelope's tea set?" she would ask one old friend after another. "You haven't? Oh, you must go along to Esselmont's and look at the display window. Penelope is teaching a class in arts and crafts in the big room at home."

This resulted, later, in my having two more pupils, both middle-aged ladies whose children had married and gone to other cities, leaving them with time on their hands.

"We must hurry home, Penelope, or your father will be screaming for his dinner, and Eric will be raiding the refrigerator," Mother said, when the stores closed and the streets began to empty. "I think I've sowed some seeds for you this afternoon, without being too commercial."

As we drove home in the rackety old car, I was dreaming of the day when I could drive up to the door in a gleaming new Lincoln or Chevrolet and say, "Dad, I've brought you a birthday present."

Wouldn't that be the day!

I drove into the garage, and Mother got out in a hurry, with her conscience hurting because we were late. As I followed her, I heard a wail, then, "Hamlet, get off! You naughty, naughty dog!"

I ran around the corner and found my mother tugging at Hamlet's collar. He was lying sprawled over Mother's tuberose begonias, the pride of her life. He just lay there, looking at Mother with puzzled eyes and not making the least attempt to get up.

"Tony," I yelled. "Tony, come and get your dog out of the flower garden. He's ruined my mother's lovely begonias."

Tony came arunning. "Here, boy! Here, Hamlet! Here, you lazy brute!"

Hamlet laid his heavy muzzle on his paws and stayed stubbornly still.

"It isn't my fault," Tony panted as he tugged at the big dog's collar. "I didn't train him, or he'd be an obedient dog. Get up, you behemoth. He's probably done all the harm he can, anyway. I'm awfully sorry, Mrs. Warburton. I can't budge him. I'm sorry he's broken your flowers, but I hope you won't blame me."

"You brought him here," I scolded. "You're responsible if anyone is."

"Don't be silly. I had to bring him here or he would have gone to a kennel and died for want of exercise."

Tony put forth all his strength and heaved the great creature to his feet and away from the garden bed. Mother knelt down and mourned over her crushed and broken begonias that were now patches of crimson and scarlet and pink and purple and yellow pulp.

Just then Dad came to the door and let out a musical bellow. "I say, are we going to have any dinner today?"

"I'll take Hamlet to my home for a few days," Tony promised. "Dad wants me to help about installing his plant.

By the way, Penelope, when are you going to let me ride
Goldie?"

"When you come back from helping your father," I said,
putting off the day. I thought he had a nerve to ask to ride
Goldie just when his Great Dane had ruined my mother's
begonias.

8

The Peach Queen

At breakfast the family discussed the plans for seeing the Peach Queen crowned.

"The Truscotts have invited me to go with them and picnic in their motorboat," I announced. I was thrilled at the prospect of a holiday, with a pageant to watch and lunch in a motorboat. It was a perfect day, as usual, and it was going to be fun.

"May I go with Gerry and Fred in Gerry's car?" Eric asked.

"I guess you may," Mother said reluctantly, "but do urge Gerry not to drive too fast."

"Your mother and I are going to Vernon to visit some of our old friends," Dad said. "I am sick to death of Peach Queens, Apple Queens, Miss Lumber Companies, Miss Mineworkers, and so forth and so on, especially Miss Universe. It isn't giving the young ladies on Venus a chance to compete."

Tony had gone home for a few days to help his father in-
stall his pottery works, so we didn't have to consider his
convenience. It was a relief to have Tony and Hamlet out
of our hair for a while.

About ten in the morning the Truscotts called for me
in their new car. Already the air was simmering. Heat
quivered above the roofs, and mirages formed on the road
ahead. I was glad we were to picnic in the boat, because it
might be slightly cooler on the water. Diana didn't seem to
mind the heat. She was used to it, but I had grown accustomed to the soft moist air near the sea, and I felt the
heat, like a polar bear in a zoo.

Already it was impossible to find a parking space near
the Aquatic Club, so Mr. Truscott had to park some distance out, and we walked on the hot sidewalks under the
blazing sun down to the boathouse where the boat was
tied. Other boat owners had the same bright idea, and the
water of Okanagan Lake was stirred by the bow waves of
speed boats and slower craft. A boat with red sails was trying to catch what little breeze there was.

We stepped aboard the boat, and two of Diana's boy
friends joined our party. Diana kindly lent me one of them.
Her dad started the outboard motor and we went merrily
down the lake. The speed of the boat made a pleasant
breeze to cool us, but still it seemed hot to me. The others
thought it was just right. Mr. Truscott tied up at a float and
let us eat our lunch. After that we cruised back to the boathouse.

"Now you young people will want to go up into town
and find yourselves a good spot to see the parade. What do
you wish to do, dear?" he asked his wife. "I intend to relax
in the Club."

"I'm going to have a swim," Mrs. Truscott replied. "It may be very remiss and dreadful of me, but I couldn't care less about seeing the Peach Queen. I've seen her around the place scores of times, and I don't suppose she'll look very different in a crown."

So we agreed on a time to be at the car, and we four walked up into the town, where crowds were already pushing about on Bernard Avenue, waiting for the procession of floats. As we were jostled about by the mob, I almost envied Mrs. Truscott swimming in the lovely cool water. If it was hot on the lake, it was ten times hotter on the street.

"You look wilted, Penelope," said a voice beside me and above me, and there was Garth Esselmont smiling down at me.

"It is kind of warm, isn't it?" I spoke cheerfully because I didn't want to grumble when I was the Truscotts' guest.

"Penelope feels the heat because she will spend ten months of the year in the rain instead of staying like a sensible girl in the valley and getting used to the sunshine," Diana teased me.

"I was going to suggest," said Garth, "that you all come up to the rooms above the store. My parents are up there, and you can sit there comfortably and watch the parade without being squashed like flies."

"Ask Diana," I said. "It's her party. Personally, I think your invitation sounds like heaven."

"Garth, you're a darling," Diana accepted. "Come on, children, follow Garth."

He led us to a side door and up a flight of stairs, and then we were in a part of the store where crates were unpacked and parcels for sending away were wrapped. Mr. and Mrs. Esselmont were sitting on folding chairs, looking out of the window. They greeted us cordially, and Garth found kitchen chairs for Diana and me and packing cases for the boys and himself.

"I hear the band," Mrs. Esselmont cried. "Here come the drum majorettes, stepping high and twirling their batons."

Some of the floats were beautiful, and it was interesting to recognize girls we knew, posing in costume on the floats. The band music was fine, and we did admire the peach float, with the Peach Queen on a throne and artificial peaches four feet long. When the parade had passed, we thanked the Esselmonts and went off to see the coronation of the Peach Queen. Garth came too, and it didn't seem to matter that we were too late to get a good view.

"You'll come home with us and stay to dinner, won't you, Penelope?" Diana coaxed when we said good-by to Garth and went to the car. "You don't want to make a teapot this evening, do you?"

"I'd love to come," I accepted. "Mother and Dad won't be home till late and Eric is off with his pals. Tony, thank goodness, is away for a few days."

Mrs. Truscott invited the two boys so that we could play tennis after dinner. We stopped in at The Poplars for me to pick up my racket and shoes.

Diana and I helped to set out a cold dinner of meat and salad and fruit. "Let's hurry," Diana urged, "so we won't be wasting daylight."

I was terribly out of practice, and I goofed so often I was embarrassed, but after the first set I got back into the swing and played a fairly good game. Then we sat on the veranda and drank lemonade and talked about the parade.

"I wouldn't want to be a Peach Queen," Diana was saying. She stopped abruptly. "Penelope, isn't that your horse?"

I nearly dropped my glass of lemonade. "It *is* Goldie!"
I cried. "Whatever can have happened?"

Goldie, saddled and bridled, was walking slowly up the
road. He looked as guilty as if he had robbed a bank. He
had heard my voice and was coming to me for protection.

"He's come to take you home," said one of the boys.

"Skipper overboard," cracked the other, who was a keen
yachtsman.

I jumped up. "This isn't funny. Someone has been thrown
and may be lying on the road, hurt. Excuse me, Diana, I
must ride back and find out."

"If his rider was lying on the road, someone would have
picked him up by this time," Diana reasoned.

"Penelope is right," the yachtsman said. "We'll run along
in our car and find out what's happened."

I ran out and mounted Goldie and was galloping along
the road before the boys had said good-by and got their
little old car to start. I was worried and I was mad. Who-
ever had been riding Goldie had done so without leave or
perhaps was trying to steal him. If Tony hadn't been away,
I'd have pinned it on him at once. I knew Eric had intended to stay in town all evening. Dad might ride my
horse if he were home and felt like a ride, but Dad would
not have been thrown. The foreman? Not likely. One of
the farm hands, taking advantage of the family's absence?
Possible, but not probable.

I watched the road anxiously and the land on either side
of the road in case the rider had been thrown clear or had
crawled or staggered off and was lying with a broken leg
among the mulleins. Then I saw Tony striding along with
his usual slight swagger, coming toward me. So, he had
come back sooner than he had intended! I was so hot I was
cold. I reined in Goldie as we met.

"Can you explain this?" I asked icily.

"Easily." Tony was as nonchalant as ever. "You said I might ride Goldie when I got back from my visit home. You weren't around, and I had nothing to do, so I saddled him and went for a ride."

I was staggered. I remembered now that I had said he might ride Goldie when he came back, but I hadn't expected him to take that as a blanket permission.

"I thought you were a good rider," I said. "Did you fall off?"

"You told me once that Goldie is a good jumper. Well, he isn't."

"You jumped him!" I gave a wail. "Did he come down on his knees?"

"No, he went over like a bird, but he rose too suddenly. I wasn't ready for it."

"So you slid off over his tail?" I was so relieved that Goldie hadn't come down on his knees that my anger cooled a bit.

"Well, yes. Goldie jumped, but I didn't. I couldn't catch him after that, so I followed him."

"I thought you had a row of cups for jumping."

"So I have." He looked sheepish. "I should have mentioned that I won them for broad jump and pole vault. It was very bad of me to give you the wrong impression."

I shut my mouth tight to keep from laughing. Tony looked sad.

"Penelope, don't be cross," he pleaded. "I can't bear it when you set your lips in a straight line and two red spots come in your cheeks, and I know I'm the culprit."

This was a completely different Tony from the cocksure, witty, impertinent student who kept me in the jitters, wondering what he would say or do next.

"If you don't like it when I'm cross, why do you keep on saying and doing things to make me cross?" I demanded. "Just for the record, why do you?"

Tony heaved a sigh too deep to be genuine. "I'm such an unpredictable chap. I never know myself where I'll break out next, and I never mean any harm. When you come right down to it, I don't do much, now, do I? Your horse is right as rain. Mrs. Bellair enjoys fighting me—it puts spice in her dull life. Anyway, half the time you imagine things, like a face on a clay dog."

By this time I couldn't keep back a giggle. "You sure have a crust to remind me of your crimes."

"Do you mean that you had forgotten them?" he asked.

"I'm going home," I said. "I hope you like walking." I put Goldie to a canter and called back over my shoulder, "Have a pleasant stroll."

I was growing bored with my Ogopogo ware, but I was stuck with it because the demand was growing. Garth Esselmont had been out twice to see how we were progressing, and he had all sorts of ideas for the Ogopogo design. He even hinted at place mats to go with a luncheon set.

An invitation to a wedding of one of my school friends gave me an excuse for a change. I made a vase of the red clay, which baked to a rich, dark brown and would be lovely for yellow or orange flowers. I gave it a clear glaze, and it was a handsome piece. I was looking forward to the wedding, late in August, for I hadn't seen anything of my school friends all summer. My pottery and my class had taken up all the bright summer days.

"You're having very little fun, Penelope, dear," Mother

said regretfully. "I'm sure Dad never expected you to drudge as you have been doing."

"It's been fun, Mother, honestly. I've really enjoyed myself. Of course, I shouldn't mind a swim or dancing or some tennis, just for exercise, but you needn't worry about me. And my piggy bank is bursting."

It really did seem as if I should be able to complete my training and get my diploma. If I could board cheaply in return for baby-sitting in the evenings, I could swing it. It would be worth putting up with the constant feuding between Tony and Mrs. Bellair. And I believe Tony was right—it added spice to Mrs. Bellair's dull life.

9

Ogopogo

Saturday was a holiday in the Penelope Craft School.
Diana invited me to drive to Penticton with her. "We've
hardly seen each other since you came home," she complained. "Your old craft school is the only thing you think
about."

"I know," I admitted. "There's been such a lot to do for
it that I haven't had much time. I'm trying to make my own
pottery for the tourist trade. Mr. Esselmont buys it from
me."

"Let's start early, before it gets too hot for you," Diana
said. "I'll call for you at eight, and we'll have a swim and
lunch in Penticton."

"Diana has invited me to go to Penticton tomorrow," I
told my mother at dinner. "Is that OK with you, Mother?"

"Has she indeed?" Mother sounded slightly cross. "I
hoped you would help me clean the house, but I suppose

I'll have to rely on Mrs. Stubbs." Mrs. Stubbs is the foreman's wife and helps Mother for a few hours every day.

"Of course you may go," Dad insisted. "The child has
been working like a horse ever since she came home. She
needs a day off."

"And I suppose I don't." Mother still sounded huffy.
She had not yet recovered from having her begonias ruined
by my pupil's dog.

"Come now, darling," Dad argued. "I'll take you for a
trip before the apple packing starts."

Wonderful holiday! I thought, to go for a trip in that old
rattletrap. To make up for going off all the next day, I
spent that entire evening cleaning the house.

Tony watched me mopping the kitchen and said with
his enraging smile, " 'Thus conscience doth make cowards
of us all.' "

"Does it affect you that way?" I asked acidly.

"I have no conscience," he replied calmly and went out.

I heard the roar of his noisemaker as he drove away. He
never mentioned where he was going.

"You're a good daughter, Penelope," Mother declared.
"I'm sorry I was stuffy."

"Mother, darling, you're never stuffy. You *do* deserve a
trip."

"Never fear," she said confidently. "I'll see that I get
one."

At eight sharp Diana was at the door in her dad's car. It
promised to be a broiling day, so we were both dressed in
blouses and shorts. Early as it was, the country was an oven.
The thermometer had stayed in the eighty-degree bracket
all night. Only the dry bracing air made the heat bearable.
As we drove, the mirages looked like pools of water on the
road ahead.

We crossed on the ferry to Westbank and saw the structure of the new bridge spanning the lake. "We may not be crossing by this ferry again," Diana remarked. "The bridge will soon be open."

As we drove along the western shore of the lake, she said, "Now, Penelope, you watch out for the Ogopogo, because I have to keep my eyes on the road."

"I don't know whether I want to see it," I demurred. "I have designed an Ogopogo for my pottery, and it might upset my ideas to see the real one. Some people claim that it only appears to boost the tourist trade. That's the time the reports come in."

"I saw it once," Diana claimed. "Naturally people see it in the early summer, because that's the time they go down to the lake to swim. I daresay it lies dormant at the bottom in cold weather."

"What did it look like" I asked.

"I only saw humpy loops, moving fast, but lots of people have seen a head like a horse's with a sort of mane."

As we drove beside Okanagan Lake, I stared hard at the rippling blue water, but I didn't see any humpy coils. On the opposite shore the dry sandy benches lay flat as if they had been made with a set square, going down with an angle of sixty degrees to the bench below. The glare hurt my eyes and I took my dark glasses out of my handbag. I hate to wear dark glasses and lose the beauty of the rich color of this country, but this day was too bright for comfort.

We drove past Peachland and around by West Summerland to see the beautiful orchards and gardens of the Government Experimental Farm. We spent some time admiring the flowers before going on to Penticton, lying in its valley at the south end of the long narrow lake.

"Shall we have a swim before lunch?" Diana asked. "Or would you like to go on to Skaha Lake?"

The waves were rolling in on the wide sandy beach, reminding me of the sea. "Oh, do let's swim here and now," I said.

It was lovely to get out of the heat and into the cool clear water. We dived and swam and had a perfectly gorgeous time. The water was not too cold. We could have stayed in all day if we hadn't begun to feel hungry.

When we were dressed, we walked up into the town and had lunch in a café. It was fun to be with Diana again, and she showed more respect for my craft work, now that I had a real class and had sold some of my pieces of pottery.

"I wonder if I'd be any good at that sort of thing," she said thoughtfully. "It would be kind of nice to make things for my house when I get married. It would be like starting heirlooms."

"I can make room for one or two more pupils," I suggested. "As a matter of fact, I'm not keen on taking on more than that because I want to have time for my Ogopogo ware."

"I'd like to see your Ogopogo ware."

"We can stop in as we go through Kelowna and see my tea set in Esselmont's window," I suggested. I was pleased to have Diana take an interest in my work. Our friendship was warming up again—though it had probably never cooled on her side nor, really, on mine.

In the afternoon we went to a show. It wasn't a very good picture, but at least it was cool in the theater. When we went back to the car, which had been parked in the shade, we found that the shade had moved and for some time the sun had been beating down on the roof. Getting into that car made me feel like pottery in the kiln. As we drove, the breeze coming in the windows was hot.

I was watching the lake for the Ogopogo and suddenly I saw, far out from shore, five undulating lumps or humps. Diana was driving fast, and I didn't want to startle her into stopping too suddenly.

"If you'd slow down a bit, I'd point out something interesting," I said. "No hurry. We can still see it."

"Not the Ogopogo?" she exclaimed as she slowed to a stop.

The creature was moving fast against the current that there is in this lake extension of a river. As suddenly as it had appeared it disappeared again.

"Gosh," said Diana, "that's the second time I've seen it. I wish we had seen the head. I wish we'd brought a camera."

"At the rate it moves, we'd need a movie camera," I remarked.

"Shall we tell anyone we saw it?" Diana asked. "I hate to be laughed at."

"I'll tell my family, because they believe that it exists."

"I guess it's our duty to tell the press," Diana murmured.

I wished then that I hadn't called Diana's attention to the lake monster, because I didn't want my name in the paper as having seen it. I don't want people to think I'm nuts.

"It would be a wonderful advertisement for your Ogopogo pottery," Diana coaxed, seeing that I didn't jump at the idea.

"Can't you say Diana Truscott and a friend saw a number of loops moving swiftly out in the lake, which they suspected to be the Ogopogo?"

"If you're afraid to back me up, we won't mention it at all." Diana's voice came straight out of the icebox. I gave in.

"OK, go ahead. The editor will probably brush you off anyway."

When we drove into the busy town, Diana went straight to the newspaper office and parked. We went in. I was feeling foolish. The editor was interested and questioned us closely.

"You're sure it wasn't a log with the waves making it look like loops?"

"The water was calm this afternoon, and the creature was moving fast against the current," Diana told him.

He made notes and thanked us for bringing in the news item. When the next edition of the paper came out, the headline read:

Two Socialites of Kelowna's Younger Set See Ogopogo

My mother was annoyed, and so was I. I'm a hard-working student and I think "socialite" is a silly word.

When we stopped at The Poplars, I tried to persuade Diana to stay to dinner. "Mother would love to have you, and you haven't been here to dinner once this summer. I'd like you to meet my freakish student. He's a scream."

"I'll take a rain check," Diana said. "I have to go home now because Mum and Dad need the car for a dinner date."

"Well, thanks a million for taking me. It's been a real treat to get away from the studio for a whole day."

"I'll come along and see the plant in operation," Diana promised before she drove away.

"Did you have a pleasant day, dear?" Mother asked

when I went to the kitchen, where she was cooking dinner.

"Out of this world. My pottery is all sold at Esselmont's, and we saw the Ogopogo."

"My dear! Did you really see the Ogopogo? What does it look like?"

"We could only see big loops moving against the current."

I went to put on a dress and then set the table and helped Mother serve dinner. I told my news during the meal, and everyone was thrilled. Even Eric treated me with respect.

"Golly, Pen, I wish I had your luck. I guess it wasn't luck selling your pottery, but it sure was luck seeing the Ogopogo."

"You all believe it *was* the Ogopogo?" I asked.

"What else could it be?" Dad shrugged. He has always been a firm believer in the existence of the strange monster, which seems to be first cousin to the Loch Ness monster and to a sea creature near Victoria.

After I had washed the dishes with Eric's usual reluctant help, I went out to the pasture to take an early apple to Goldie. I climbed the fence and whistled. No Goldie came. I could not see him in the pasture. Then I noticed that the gate was open.

Goldie is a clever horse, and long ago he learned to lift the hook from the staple and open the gate. So we put on a padlock. I used to leave the key in the padlock, so that Dad and the farm hands could go in without any trouble. Now I was sure that someone who didn't know that the hook was Goldie's toy had opened and closed the pasture gate. I went back to the house in a temper.

"Who let Goldie out of the pasture?" I stormed in a voice that carried all over the house.

"I didn't." That was from Eric, lying on the couch with a motor magazine.

"I didn't imagine you had, but he's out and the gate was left unlocked. I'm going to ask Dad to go down the road in the car."

I went out to look for Dad and found Tony playing games with a ball and that great elephant of a dog.

"Have you seen my father?" I asked. "Someone has opened the pasture gate and Goldie is away and gone."

Tony turned red. "I say . . . I borrowed Goldie for a short ride—you know you said I might—but I put him back in the pasture and closed the gate. I know I did."

"How did you fasten the gate?" I asked. I was pretty vexed at his having taken my horse a second time without definite leave.

"I distinctly remember putting the large hook into the staple," he answered. "I'm positive I did."

"I'm sure you did," I nodded. "That hook-and-staple catch is child's play to Goldie. Didn't you notice you had to unlock a padlock to get in? Will you please not ride Goldie again?"

I left him to think that one over while I went to find Dad.

10

Wong Kee's Wheel

Dad and I went in the car and drove along the main road in one direction and then in the other, stopping now and then to make inquiries, but no one had seen a palomino astray. We began to go up side roads until after an hour's driving we found his lordship in an orchard with alfalfa growing between the rows of fruit trees. I got out of the car and whistled to him. To my dismay he kicked up his heels and galloped away. He had tasted liberty and stolen alfalfa and was in a mood of rebellion.

I went to the grower's house to apologize for my horse's raid and offer to pay for any damage he had done.

"He has always come to my whistle," I told the grower, "but this time he has eaten so much of your good alfalfa that I don't believe he would come even for a pan of oats. I don't know how to catch him."

"I don't keep livestock," said the grower, "so no oats. We'll have to try to head him off."

Goldie had stopped galloping around and was chomping

alfalfa when I walked quietly up to him and grabbed his mane. In an instant I had the bridle over his head. "Bit," I said crossly, for I was feeling considerably ruffled. He took his bit in his usual obedient way, and in another instant I was on his back. The grower brushed off my offer to pay for the damage.

Dad drove the car home, and I followed on my escapee. I was scared he might get colic from eating too much juicy alfalfa when he's used to pasture grass and a small ration of oats. Dad waited at the stable until I rode in. "I think I'll keep him in the stable and not water him until tomorrow morning," I said. "I'm scared of colic."

"You're just as wise," Dad agreed. "I'll stay up and take a look at him around midnight. I'm not worried about the horse, but I *am* fed up with that zany pupil of yours, with his giant of a dog lying on your mother's flowers, and his earthshaking car, and his free-and-easy ways."

"Me, too," I sighed, "but I can't expel him."

Next morning Tony was so penitent and subdued that I had to forgive him. "I yielded to an overwhelming temptation to ride Goldie again," he confessed. "I rode about a mile along the road and back and let him loose in the pasture again. I had forgotten about the padlock and I just dropped the hook in the staple. It never entered my mind that Goldie could lift the hook."

So I forgave him and hoped he would simmer down for a while. I was uneasy for fear Mrs. Bellair would hear about his escapade and make snide remarks.

That was the day Wong Kee drifted in to see my pottery. Wong Kee was employed in the orchard when Dad bought the place. Five years ago he retired, and Dad lets him live rent free in the log shack he had always lived in. There he putters in a small tidy vegetable garden and collects junk.

He's an inventor. Out of the junk he contrives tools, gadgets, and even machinery. Whenever any part of the sprayer breaks down, Wong Kee is on hand with a spare part. He built himself a small pick-up truck in which he rumbles along the roads looking for more junk.

Luckily Wong Kee is very tidy and keeps his junk neatly stored in a lean-to shed of his shack. His two rooms are spotlessly trim, and his bed is covered by a white sheet, smoothly tucked in. He wears blue jeans and a cardigan sweater and always looks clean and well mended. With his old-age pension he is well off and is saving money to bring his grandson over from China. The gift he most appreciates is a pot of preserved ginger. When I come home from Vancouver, I always bring him something from a Chinese store—ginger, lichi nuts, or Chinese tea, and he says I am a good mother to him.

Wong Kee was excited when he heard about my pottery. In China he had often watched his uncle at work making crude crockery. This morning he inspected all the work with keen interest, making comments, some complimentary and some the reverse. He watched me modeling a cup.

"I show you how makee horse," he said. He picked up a small lump of clay and started work. His hands are so gnarled and seamed that they looked as though he would fumble, but he didn't. His brown parchment face, wrinkled like milk coming to the boil, was intent, his little black eyes slits as he worked.

In Chinese antique shops I have seen the eight immortal horses, so when Wong Kee placed his figurine on the table, I recognized one of them. "That's an immortal horse." The old man beamed and clucked.

"You must come in when you feel like it and show us how to make Chinese horses and dogs," I said.

"You wantee wheel," he said. "I make."

"That would be great, Wong Kee." I half believed he could do it.

The class laughed when the old man had shuffled out of the door. I shook my head. "You needn't laugh yet. I'm not sure he won't do it. He's a great old inventor."

"You'd do better to write to some of the addresses I gave you, Penelope," Tony predicted. "You stand a better chance of getting a wheel."

"I've written to two of them," I answered. "We'll wait and see."

A day or two later I had replies from the antique and second-hand stores. They were sorry, but they were unable to supply a potter's wheel.

The following day there was a thumping and a grunting outside, and the foreman knocked at the studio door. "Excuse me, Miss Warburton, but Wong Kee has a contraption here he says he promised you."

"Oh, yes." I was flabbergasted by what I saw. "Bring it in, please. Wong Kee, this is kind of you. Thank you very much."

Wong Kee had combed over his collection of junk and had invented a potter's wheel such as has never been seen before. He had used primitive ideas and modern machinery in a fantastic combination. The wheel had once been a grindstone. The treadle and the frame had once been parts of the sewing machine I had seen in his pick-up the day I came home.

Wong Kee sat down and demonstrated how the wheel would spin when he worked the treadle. "You makee foot go fast, wheel go fast. Makee foot go slow, wheel go slow."

I could see that he had made a strong frame to hold the weight of the grindstone. I gave him a ball of clay. Though it was sixty years since he had watched his uncle, he had not forgotten the technique. He dipped his hands in the basin of water, threw the ball in the center of the wheel, and began to pedal slowly while with his two hands he shaped a bowl. I stood by with scrapers, leather, and cutting wire, like a nurse handing instruments to a surgeon. When the bowl was ready, I gave him the wire to cut it off the disk and a small board to move it onto carefully.

"I'll bake it and glaze it for you with my next batch," I promised. "It can hold your rice."

All the class had gathered around to watch the old man demonstrate his wheel. He was so pleased with it that I was scared he would go on all day. When his bowl was finished, he let me have a turn.

"Good?" he asked, glowing with pride.

"Very good," I told him, and all the class praised him till he was almost dizzy with joy.

"I go now," he said at last. "You bake, makee good for me eat lice, eat soup, eat egg in soup, eat gleen peas." He chuckled and rubbed the clay off his hands. "I go now. Good-by." He gave his bowl a fond look as he went slowly out.

"You win, Penelope." Tony laughed. "The thing really works, doesn't it?"

"You all want to take a turn, I'm sure," I said. "You'll have to take turns alphabetically. Mrs. Bellair, Doreen, Lyn, Pat, Susan. Tony, you're the last."

"You've taken us all by our first names except Mrs. Bellair," Tony protested. "That isn't fair. I'd come earlier in the game if we all had surname initials."

"I don't care, I'm the same either way," Susan said.

"And I would be first if you used my given name," Mrs. Bellair announced, "because my first name is Annabel."

The whole day was spent in trying out Wong Kee's wheel. As I had predicted, the only disadvantage to a potter's wheel is that everyone wants it at the same time.

During the noon hour I was called to the telephone. "Garth Esselmont speaking. Dad wants to know if you have any more Ogopogo ware ready."

"I have a set of bowls in the biscuit, but they need to be glazed and baked again. I'm afraid I won't have any ready this week. I had a great surprise this morning; Wong Kee, the old Chinese gardener who lives in the orchard, brought me in a potter's wheel he made out of junk."

"Holy mackerel! Does it work?"

"Like a charm. Wong Kee sat right down and modeled a bowl for his rice."

"This I must see. May I come out this afternoon?"

"We'll be glad to see you."

I thought it strange that Garth should be able to take an hour or so out from his father's store just to see a potter's wheel made by an old Chinese gardener. I surmised that he hoped to pick up some pottery or weaving for the gift section of the store. When I went back to the table, Eric asked, "Are you getting another pupil, Pen? You look like you'd come into a fortune."

"You look as though—not like—Eric," Mother corrected him. "Don't murder the English language."

"Esselmont's store is hot on the trail of more Ogopogo ware," I spoke to Mother, ignoring my brother. "While I'm teaching, I can't keep up with the demand, but that's a good deal better than not having demand, isn't it?"

"I think that's very encouraging," Mother said.

"You're onto a good racket, Penelope," Dad added.

"Do you allow Dad to murder the English language,

Mum?" Eric asked impudently. I never knew a boy to be so brash.

"Your father was using a figure of speech, Eric," Mother said firmly. "You were merely using an ungrammatical term."

Eric subsided, and I quickly started to talk about Wong Kee's potter's wheel and to describe the old man's pride and his bowl.

"What color will you glaze it?" Mother asked.

"I'll be glazing my stuff pale green, so I'll probably do his bowl the same."

After lunch I put on a clean smock, a new one without any paint or glaze stains on it. It was a pretty shade of blue, which suits me better than my old tan smocks. Tony noticed it at once.

"Teacher is all dolled up," he remarked to no one in particular. "Teacher doesn't expect a visitor to the studio, does she?"

I decided to ignore him, just as I had ignored Eric, but of course everyone looked up and stared at me and my new smock.

"It's a pretty color," Doreen remarked. "I guess I'll buy a flowered smock with a gray background that won't show the clay so much. I have a dreadful habit of wiping my hands on my smock."

"Let's all buy flowered smocks," Tony suggested. "We'll make the studio look like a flower garden."

"No one would ever mistake you for a flower, Mr. Lestrange," Mrs. Bellair sneered.

"My harmless joke seems to have annoyed Mrs. Bellair," Tony mused aloud. "I'd be wise to keep my trap shut."

"I wonder that anyone so deeply in disgrace as you

would dare to open it," Mrs. Bellair said with a sharp, cackling laugh.

Tony turned a deep red. "I know now what Solomon meant when he said that the laughter of fools is like the crackling of thorns under a pot," he said in an undertone to Doreen. I heard him plainly, but I hoped the clacking of the big loom had screened his insulting remark from Mrs. Bellair's ears. Trying to keep a shooting war from breaking out between those two was making me a nervous wreck.

I wondered how Mrs. Bellair had heard about Goldie's escape. The grapevine is a busy social service in the country. I didn't want Tony to think I had tattled.

"I don't know why you say that Tony is in disgrace, Mrs. Bellair," I said. "He isn't in disgrace with me, and I have never said anything to anyone to suggest such a thing."

Mrs. Bellair tossed her head. "You needn't snub me, Penelope. I heard how Goldie got out of the pasture."

"That was just a misunderstanding. Tony didn't know what a clever horse Goldie is, and he had asked my permission to ride him some day." I could have throttled the old lady. "Who wants a turn at the potter's wheel?" I asked brightly. "Come early and avoid the rush."

The work went humming along, but I was shaking so that I could hardly shape the clay. If things got much worse between Mrs. Bellair and Tony, I didn't know what I should do. Mrs. Bellair was here first, but if Tony were asked to leave I couldn't refund his fee, for I had given the money to Dad. I began to wish I had never started this class. I guess every fresh venture has its snags.

It was a relief when there was a knock at the door and I opened it to let Garth in. "Hi, Penelope," he said with a smile. "Esselmont's Store sent me to scout around for more pottery and place mats. How is it coming?"

"Come and talk to my pupils." I tried to sound surprised.
"I'm afraid my stuff is only in the biscuit yet, but Pat Terry
has a set of place mats, haven't you, Pat? And some of the
others have figurines and ashtrays. You must see the potter's wheel Wong Kee has made for me."

"You don't tell me! Well, this is something unique."
Garth sat down and worked the pedal to spin the wheel.
"By cracky! This is fantastic, utterly fantastic. Where did
he get the unrelated parts?"

I laughed. "Collecting junk is Wong Kee's hobby. He
makes all sorts of things out of his junk, but this is the most
original."

Garth looked over all the work and bought several
pieces. I was glad my pupils were able to sell stuff to prove
that their course was worthwhile financially. Pat Terry was
especially pleased because it meant so much to him to be
able to help his mother with her finances. Only Doreen de-
clined to sell anything because she was making things only
for herself and for gifts. Mrs. Bellair didn't have a chance
to decline, for her work was consistently poor. She kept
making little dogs attached to trays, and they were terrible.

I found a carton for Garth to pack his purchases in, and
he asked me to open the front door for him to carry the box
out.

"I didn't actually need you to open the door," he said.
"I wanted a chance to ask you to go for a drive this evening.
I've bought a second-hand Studebaker, last year's model,
and I'd like your opinion of it."

"I'll be thrilled, though my opinion of a car is not worth
the breath it's spoken with. What time shall I be ready?"

"Is seven too early? I thought we might cruise along up
to the Belgo and along the John Oliver road and round by
the Mission Creek road, out of the traffic."

"I'll be ready," I promised.

When I went back to my class, Tony and Pat glared at me accusingly, though they had both sold items to Garth. The girls were in a flutter.

"Isn't it marvelous to have Esselmont's send a buyer out to scout—actually scout—for our work?" Doreen caroled. "We have to thank your tea set for that."

"Isn't Garth handsome?" Lyn sighed. "Oh, I think he's the cutest thing."

"I wish I'd had something made for sale," Susan complained. "I never seem to have the luck to get things finished in time."

"He evidently has no eye for art unless it's functional," Mrs. Bellair sniffed. "He didn't so much as glance at my sweet little dogs."

"He can't buy too much at one time," I tried to console her. "But it's a market that will probably expand as our work gets known. It serves you right, Susan, because you're too lazy to finish a piece. You always want to start something new, and then get tired of it, and drop it."

"If you had found time to bake the darling little pekingese I made last week . . ." Mrs. Bellair began.

"You would have had one more animal for Esselmont to ignore," Tony finished her sentence for her. Lyn giggled. I glared at her and then at Tony.

At dinner Mother lifted her eyebrows at my new green nylon. "Are you going to a party this evening, dear?"

"No, but Garth Esselmont is coming to take me for a drive in the car he has just bought. He's coming at seven, so I dressed before dinner so as to have time to wash the dishes. I'll put on a large apron."

"What make has he bought?" Eric was more interested in the car than in my dress. "What year?"

"Last year's Studebaker."

"It's not much use taking you out to try it. You don't know the difference between a sports car and a hot rod. Maybe he'd like me to tag along and tell him what's wrong with it."

Eric has the best ideas. "Maybe he wouldn't want to hear what's wrong with it," I squashed him. "Any garage can tell him that."

"This Garth fellow mixes pleasure with business," Tony remarked. "He's taken a sudden violent interest in craft work. I suspect he admires Doreen." He looked at me with a wicked glint in his eyes. "She lives in Kelowna, and he probably dates her there."

"Don't worry about the dishes, dear," Mother said. "I've been gadding all afternoon while you were working, so I'll wash the dishes and Eric will dry, won't you, Eric, darling?"

"I'm 'Eric, darling' when I'm wanted to dry the dishes, and I'm 'that boy' when I try to sneak out," Eric said in a sulky tone.

"Well, then you know how to stay in the darling class." Mother gave him her sweetest smile.

I was walking on air. My class was producing salable stuff, and handsome Garth Esselmont was coming to take me for a drive. Tony could go jump in the lake.

11

Palette and Film

I was ready when Garth drove up to the door at five minutes past seven. The car was gleaming, and the cushioned seat was a dream of luxury after our knobby old car springs. We drove away toward Black Mountain.

As we drove down the long grade from the Belgo, the sun was slanting through the trees beside the road and turning the distant lake into a blade of burnished steel. The wide valley spread out below us.

"I love this drive when the orchards are all in bloom and smelling heavenly," I remarked. "I've missed that sight for three years. I haven't come home until the blossom was over, and I've gone again before the apples were ripe. It's gorgeous now, when the air is filled with golden haze. I've never seen country where the air turns golden in the early evening, except this valley."

"You sound poetical. It's the dust from the sandy hills,"

Garth said practically. "It certainly does have a magical effect, like the light in some famous paintings."

When we reached the Vernon road, I thought Garth would turn homeward, but he swung out on the highway and kept straight on, if you could call it straight on such a winding road. Twelve miles from Kelowna we came to Kalamalka Lake. The water, deep blue-green, reflected the tawny hills on the opposite shore.

"I always think those hills look like cougars crouching. I must come up some day and paint the view in oils. The colors are so strong that they need oils."

"Let's make a date for Sunday afternoon," Garth said.

"We have a service in our own little church on Sunday afternoon," I was struggling with my conscience.

"We could go right after the service and take a picnic basket. I'll bring my camera with some color film and see which comes out best."

I laughed. "I know which will come out biggest."

"Mine will be biggest when it's thrown on a screen by Dad's projector."

When we reached Oyama, I said, "I think we should turn back now, Garth. Mother will be worrying."

"It's not late, but if you say so, we'll go back. Is it a date for Sunday?"

Now, all of a sudden I was a little bit scared. I wanted to say yes and I wanted to paint Kalamalka Lake, but I held back half nervously.

"I don't know what Mother will say about my going out with you twice in one week. Mother is old-fashioned in some ways."

Garth didn't answer. I had expected him to coax, and when he looked at the road ahead and didn't reply, I was scared it would turn out that I wouldn't go on Sunday.

After a while he said, "I don't want to get in dutch with your mother, but you might at least ask her and phone me if you will go. It was your idea that you wanted to paint Kalamalka Lake, and I was anxious to oblige."

"Did you think I was hinting?" I cried, dismayed.

"Certainly not, silly girl. I was glad of a chance to do something for you. You're so self-sufficient, with your art and your pupils that you don't give a fellow a chance to know you."

"I'm sorry, Garth." I was sorrier than I wanted to let on. "My old pal Diana is peeved because I have so little time to see her, and I haven't even said hello to my other friends. I guess it's no secret that Dad took a beating with the apple crop last year, and if I don't make good with my class and so on, I don't go to art school for my last year. No school, no diploma."

"I see," Garth answered slowly. "I can see you'd want to get your diploma. I'm a busy guy myself. Dad's store is swarming with tourists, and there's plenty of work behind the scenes, buying china and gifts and supplies, like wrapping paper, and packing and unpacking. I keep the accounts, too, and I often work till midnight."

"I appreciate your taking time out to visit my class. It's given them a real lift, especially Pat Terry. He's crazy to earn money and not be dependent on his mother."

"Well, what about Sunday?" Garth went back to the starting point.

"I'll come, and thanks a million for giving me a chance to paint this scene."

We were being guarded and stuffy, talking so carefully and so politely. What was the matter with us all of a sudden?

We stopped at a place with a glorious view. "Do you

want to get out and walk to the edge?" Garth asked. "It would be a good view for a picture."

"There used to be rattlesnakes here," I said cautiously. "I guess I won't get out."

"I should think the traffic has scared the rattlers away," Garth said and drove on.

"That's one thing about Vancouver," I remarked, just to make conversation, "no rattlesnakes, no mosquitoes, no black widow spiders."

"Would you like to live there all the year round?" Garth asked.

"No. I like the sunshine in the valley and the fruit trees and the air that makes you feel like dancing. But I'd like to spend a few weeks in Vancouver every year."

"I wanted to get my degree at the university, you know, but I had to help Dad out," Garth confided.

"Did you like the university life?" I asked.

"Ah, did I?" Garth's tone was nostalgic. "I lived on the campus, and I managed to horn in on every interesting activity I could. I attended concerts and plays and lectures in the evenings, and I swam and fenced. I sure crammed a lot of fun into those three years."

The stuffy feeling was gone now, and we could talk about drama and art collections and the sculpture on the campus lawns and all sorts of things, for I often went to plays and art exhibitions at the university.

"It's funny we didn't bump into each other on the campus," I remarked. "I was often there during your third year."

"Nine thousand students, and we were probably in different buildings at the same time," Garth presumed. "I wish we had."

By the time Garth stopped the car in front of my home,

we had much in common. "Come in and have a cup of coffee," I said.

Later, when Garth said good night, he reminded me, "I'll call for you on Sunday, then."

After he had gone, Mother asked, "Where are you planning to go on Sunday? The rector is coming from Kelowna to hold a service in our church."

"I know, Mother. We're going after that. I said I would like to paint a view of Kalamalka Lake, and Garth kindly offered to drive me up there."

"Hm," said my mother, "very kind of him."

On Sunday I had my easel and stool, palette and paintbox ready, with a vacuum bottle of coffee and a basket of sandwiches and plums, all hidden in a closet under the stairs. I sort of hoped Eric wouldn't go there to look for anything. My easel folds up, so, when Garth arrived in his new car, I was able to pack all my dunnage in the trunk, beside Garth's camera and tripod.

This time we took the direct route, with the one idea of having time for pictures while the light was right. We found a place we both liked, where there was room to park and never mind if there were rattlesnakes. I set up my easel and an oil board. I knew there would be only time for a sketch, and I wouldn't stretch a canvas for it.

"Hold it," Garth ordered, as I started to draw in the scene. "There. That's going to be the best picture in this roll of films."

He wandered off then, looking for views to take in color photography. No photographer could ask for more vivid color. The lake, so I've been told, has some minerals in the water that give it the vivid blue-green, and the contrast between the lake and the yellow-tawny sand hills is spectacular. The hills are such strange shapes and the sky

so intensely blue that the whole scene looks more like a
modern painting or stage set than real nature. I knew that
I could paint it just as it is, and yet it would look like a back-
drop in a little theater.

While I splashed on the color and stressed the design of
the folds of yellow hills, Garth took pictures of me from
various angles, as I learned later. I was too much absorbed
in my work to notice what he was doing.

When the light changed, I had to stop. Garth came to
inspect my sketch. "Strong," he commented. "Of course it
had to be. There's nothing weak about this scenery."

"You like?" I was almost afraid to ask.

"Sure I like," he replied as if he really meant it. "You've
found the design, the pattern of the lines of the hills, and
your color is good. But, say, I'm hungry."

He folded up his tripod and stowed it and his camera in
the trunk of the car. "Let's sit in the back seat and eat our
supper."

Garth had brought little sausage rolls that his mother
had made and chocolate éclairs, so between us we did very
well. The hot coffee was just what we needed.

"You're lucky," Garth said. "You can see your picture,
but I have to wait to get mine developed. I finished the
roll, so I'll drop them in at the studio tomorrow, and the
films will be ready the next day. That guy has a quick
process. I'll bring them out to show you and bring my
viewer. If you like, I could bring my dad's projector and a
screen."

"Oh, I wouldn't want you to take so much trouble," I
said, feeling scared again.

"No trouble at all. I just stow them in the trunk of my
car. Remind me to ask you how you like my car."

"I love it."

"Rides easily, doesn't she?"

"Like riding on a cloud."

A little smile quirked his lips. "A pink cloud?"

"I hadn't thought about the color. Speaking of color, do you notice a thing about the shadows in this valley? They're black and solid. At the coast the shadows are transparent and filled with colors."

"I hadn't noticed, but then I don't try to interpret; I only rely on the light meter. After this I'll observe. Artists have to observe more than photographers, don't they?"

Garth was turning his head to gaze at me, and it was disconcerting. When people look very hard at me, I feel self-conscious because I know I'm no film star. If I must be looked at, I prefer it to be a fleeting glance.

"I'm sure I got some lovely pictures today," he said. "I can hardly wait to see them."

"Let's go home and show my sketch to my parents. *I* can hardly wait to hear their opinion and know the worst."

I put the empty vacuum bottle into the empty basket and got out of the back seat and into the seat beside the driver's.

"Hold on," Garth said laughing, "Wouldn't you like to drive the pink cloud for a while and see how nicely she answers the wheel?"

"Will you really trust me? Oh, Garth, I haven't driven anything but our ancient Ford, and I may not be able to navigate on this curving road."

"Sure you will. Slide over and take the wheel."

I slid over and Garth got in beside me. I was really scared, because the dashboard and all the gadgets looked so alarming. I started very slowly, and cars whizzed past me all the time. Even when I had the feel of it, I was afraid to drive faster than thirty because of the many curves.

"It's a peach of a car to drive," I said. "I can imagine that when you're used to it, you'll find it a real pleasure."

Garth laughed. "I hope you'll get used to it . . . soon."

When I showed my sketch to my family, it took them a little while to understand it. "That's great, Pen," Eric said. "You've caught the rhythm of the hills."

I gave him a grateful look.

"It's Kalamalka Lake exactly," Dad said.

"It makes a striking picture," Mother admitted. Corot is her favorite landscape artist.

Sure enough, in the middle of the week Garth arrived one evening with his dad's projector, a screen, and his own color films. "Could we show them in your studio?" he asked. "Or is it too light there?"

"The living room would be better," Mother said, "and we can pull the drapes to make it dark enough."

Businesslike and professional, Garth set up his screen and his projector and arranged chairs for his audience, which consisted of my family, Tony, the foreman and his wife, Bill and Doug, and Wong Kee. Garth turned on the light and put in a film. It showed a crowd of holiday makers on the beach in Kelowna, and the colors were brilliant.

"Ki-yi-yi!" exclaimed Wong Kee. "You makee allee same movie house."

"Only trouble is my pictures don't move," Garth laughed.

"They certainly glow," I said. "They looked brighter than life."

"I can recognize Alan and Audrey and Gerry," Eric said.

Garth drew out the film and put in another. I was perfectly happy while he showed pictures of views and animals. When he came to the films he had taken on Sunday, I grew more and more confused. I wished I hadn't invited anyone outside of the family. Picture after picture showed Penelope Warburton painting, seen from the right, seen from the left, seen with the lake as background, seen with the Studebaker as background, seen squeezing a tube of paint.

Eric started to chuckle. "You sure wasted a lot of footage on Penelope."

"It isn't often you get anyone to pose without knowing it," Garth answered calmly. "That light-green dress made a spot of pale color against all the strong colors of that scene."

His explanation sounded reasonable, but the air tingled with unspoken comments. Wong Kee put the feeling into words.

"Ki-yi-yi! Mister Eslmon, you go for catchee Miss Plenope for wife?"

Everyone laughed nervously, and I guess I sounded slightly hysterical. Garth put in a film of his car, with himself standing beside it. "You've got something there, Wong Kee," he said casually. "That's all, folks. That's the end."

"Thank you very much, Garth," Mother said. "That was truly entertaining."

The foreman and his wife and the two men said their thanks and went out, followed by Wong Kee. I escaped to the kitchen to make coffee, while Garth folded up the screen and put the projector in its case. When I brought the coffee tray in, Garth was looking at Eric's camera and advising him about taking color pictures.

"Color films are so darned expensive," Eric complained.

"And if you want to have prints, you need to be in the chips."

"You have to be sure you have an interesting picture before you shoot," Garth cautioned. "Some camera fiends just go click-click-click, and when they show their film with a projector, they bore you stiff. The great thing is to be selective."

"I've noticed that," Dad agreed. "I spent a tedious evening recently, wondering how a man could take a trip in fascinating country and come home with such a collection of dull pictures."

"Me standing in front of the Peace Arch. I set the timer and put myself in the picture, but I got it too low and the Peace Arch doesn't show much. Me and the wife beside a pyramid . . . that's my wife on the left . . ." Tony gave a hilarious imitation of a flat speaker showing tame pictures. "My wife smelling a flower. Our table set for Christmas dinner. Our camp. That's my brother-in-law holding up a fish, the one in the plaid shirt."

"You must admit they're pleasant reminders of good times," Mother kindly suggested.

"They should be kept for family use only," Dad argued. "Camera addicts have no right to inflict spiceless pictures on captive guests."

"But your pictures are really interesting and selective, Garth," Mother said quickly.

Altogether too selective, I thought, with my ears still burning from Wong Kee's observation.

12

Tony's Troubles

When I faced my class the next morning, I knew I was in for a bad day. The moccasin telegraph had been in operation. Tony was moody; Pat Terry looked reproachful. Mrs. Bellair gave it words, in her thin high voice.

"I hear you figure in some fine color photography, Penelope." She gave the little cackle she uses for a laugh. "You appear to have made a conquest. Young Esselmont seems quite *épris*. I'm sure your class won't object, if they continue to sell their little pots. It's useful to have a friend at court."

I hate it when Mrs. Bellair uses French terms, because it always means she is saying something she won't come right out and say in English.

"My French is rusty, Mrs. Bellair," I said, "but you can be sure the Esselmont store won't buy anything that isn't attractive enough to sell at a good profit. I'm hoping for the day when we'll be so famous that all our customers will buy direct from us, and we can cut out the middleman. You can do it if you try."

"I'd take great pleasure in cutting out Garth Esselmont," Tony said grimly.

"Don't let's get personal, Tony," I said.

"Give me my fur earmuffs," Tony said, "before the icicle in your voice penetrates my brain."

"It would take a power drill to do that," Mrs. Bellair purred.

"We're not famous yet," I said, and I could feel my cheeks blazing. "We'll be glad enough to sell to Esselmont's store until our work is a darned sight more distinguished than it is at present."

> "The fishes answered with a grin
> Why, what a temper you are in."

That was Tony, of course, with one eyebrow lifted and those mischievous quirks at the corners of his mouth. I shot right back at him from the same poem:

> "I sent to them again to say
> It will be better to obey."

"Touché." Tony laughed. "Let's all kiss and make friends. Come and help me get this curve right, there's a dear good teacher."

That was Tony all over. He could drive you to distraction and then with a spray of his charm make you feel silly for being vexed. For a few minutes I helped him to make his curve more beautiful, and then I went around inspecting everyone's work, and the class settled down.

I felt shaken by the small flare-up. Some people revel in a

good old knock-down-drag-out, but not this little one. I am a peace lover and probably a coward. I grew calmer as I saw what good work my pupils were doing, considering the short time they had been learning crafts. Even Mrs. Bellair worked hard, poor soul, but she insisted on walking before she could creep. She would not learn the basic principles, and often as not her pieces cracked while they were drying.

I was working every evening, making pieces for sale, and my kiln was baking one load after another. It was lucky for me that my pupils were slow and varied their work by weaving and making leather wallets, so I was able to bake my own stuff fairly often. I desperately needed a larger kiln, but it would have been too costly.

Dad came into the studio while I was at work one evening. "How are your finances, Penelope?" he asked diffidently.

"Pretty fair, Dad," I said cautiously. I had said I wanted to help with expenses, but I knew how money could sink out of sight in an orchard, and I did hope to cache enough for my final year.

"I hate to bother you," Dad went on, "but I had to leave the car at the garage for repairs, and the bill will come to more than I expected. It's sixty-five dollars. I ought not to have had the work done, I suppose, but I hate to take your mother driving in the truck. Anyway, the truck needs new tires."

So, pop! went sixty-five dollars.

"I'll return it to you when the cherry payments are made," Dad promised. I knew that when the cherry payments were made, the bank would want the loan repaid and other expenses would swoop down on us. I began to feel discouraged.

Next day there was a telephone call for Tony while we were at lunch. The telephone is in the hall, and if the door is left open, people at the table can't help hearing what is said. As a family we have no secrets, so we don't mind. Tony's voice came so loud and clear that, though we tried to cover up with chat, every word reached us.

"Tony Lestrange speaking . . . Sure, I'll come at once. This is a real blow to me. He's been such a wonderful pal to me. Life will be a lonelier journey . . . Yes, yes . . . I'll try not to grieve . . . it's one of the 'shocks that flesh is heir to' . . . I'll be with you in half an hour."

Our faces were growing long. "He must have heard of the death of a great friend," I whispered to Dad.

"I'm afraid it's his father," Dad muttered. "Overworked himself building his pottery probably."

Tony came back to the table, drooping in every line and trailing his table napkin, the picture of misery. We all gave him sympathetic looks. Mother said nervously, "I trust you haven't heard bad news, Tony?"

"You're right, I have," Tony answered dolefully. "Very bad news." He slumped into his chair. "I'm losing Hamlet. The chap who owns him has come back and wants him. I have to take him to Kelowna right away."

All our faces went back to their proper cheerful shapes, and our knives and forks started working again.

"You'll miss him," Mother said happily, "but it would be a pity to get too attached to a dog that didn't belong to you."

"I have got too attached to old Hamlet," Tony replied mournfully. "You are probably congratulating yourself that he won't be lying on your flowerbeds any more."

"Oh, no," Mother said guiltily. "He's a very good-natured dog. He got on perfectly with Mac."

"A handsome fellow," Dad remarked. "I suppose he's worth about a thousand dollars."

"That's the price his owner refused," Tony replied.

"You had a nerve to take on the job of looking after a valuable dog when you didn't know what kind of place you were coming to," Eric blurted out. "We might have been dog haters, or we might have had a bulldog that would kill him."

"In this life one has to take some chances," Tony defended himself. " 'All's well that ends well' or at best fairly well. Some day I may be able to buy myself a Great Dane pup."

He excused himself then and went out to find Hamlet and let him jump into the Tatraplan, where he sat looking around like royalty. After volcanic rumblings, the car bounded forward, and Hamlet went out of our lives.

Tony came home in about an hour, bringing a parcel for Mother. "It's not exactly the same as the one Hamlet ruined," he apologized, "but I bought the nearest to it I could find. I drove three sales clerks to gibbering lunacy before I was satisfied."

Mother opened the parcel and took out a pink candlewick counterpane, much better than one Hamlet had spoiled.

"Oh, Tony, you shouldn't have done this," she protested. "It was only an old coverlet that Hamlet had messed up a little bit."

Certainly Tony was unpredictable.

Tony came to dinner that evening looking very dejected, but there was a leg of lamb with mint sauce and early potatoes and green peas and cherry tomatoes, all the vegetables out of our own garden, and honeydew melon out of our hotbed, and by the time Mother poured the coffee, Tony was looking cheerful again.

"There are compensations." He threw the remark into the air without any connection with the subject we were discussing. "One is that I'll have more time for practicing."

"Don't overwork," Mother advised. "You should relax in the evening."

"Oh, practicing is relaxation of a sort," Tony said vaguely.

I was thinking that he had better not try to practice with the potter's wheel, because I planned to use it myself this evening. Mother is always coaxing me to take it easy in the evening, but it is the only time I can be sure of having the wheel.

I needn't have worried about the wheel. After dinner Tony went up to his room. In a few minutes we heard a rasping, grating noise that penetrated every room in the house.

"Tony tuning his violin," Eric interpreted. "Ouch!"

In a minute Tony seemed to be satisfied that his instrument of torture was in tune, and he began to play scales and what must have been exercises, for they had no tune in them. It sounded more like someone filing a saw then anything else I had ever heard. I once heard a Swedish logger playing on a saw with a violin bow, and it sounded better than Tony's violin. I guess that's why loggers call a bucking saw a Swedish violin.

"So that's what we've traded Hamlet for," I moaned.

Mother came out to the kitchen. "Penelope, will he keep that up all evening? Your father has had the car repaired. Would it be nice to invite Tony to go to the beach for a swim?"

"It sounds like a solution, but," I shook my head, "I doubt if he'll accept. He can go for a swim any time he likes, driving his own car."

"Having company might appeal to him, or he might like to be invited. Will you come too, Penelope?"

"I'd like nothing better, but it's my chance to use the potter's wheel when everyone in the class isn't clamoring for it."

"I'll wait a little while. Maybe he'll stop of his own accord when he realizes what horrible noises he's making. In half an hour, if he hasn't stopped, I'll go and ask him. We have to wait an hour after a meal before swimming, anyway."

Tony finished his scales and exercises and went on to a sort of tune, which was worse in a way, because we could almost recognize what he was trying to play, and then it would slither away from us.

"I'll go and wash the car," Eric said. "Not that it's much use. It will be dusty again by the time we get to town."

I took an early apple out to Goldie and stayed for a while, talking to him and petting him. "It must be nearly half an hour," I told him. "I must go back now, Goldie, old boy. Probably Mother has succeeded in coaxing him to go for a swim."

Before I was even near the house, I could hear the screech of the violin coming from Tony's window. When I went into the house, I heard Mother tapping at his door. The grinding noise ceased, and Tony's voice said, "Come in."

"We're just going to run down to the Aquatic Club for a swim, Tony. Would you care to come with us?" Mother's tones were sweet and liquid as a ruffed grouse's call in the spring. I held my breath for Tony's answer.

"Thanks immensely, Mrs. Warburton." His clear tones came floating down the stair well. "It's kind of you to think of me, but I'm obliged to learn to play this darned old fiddle, and I'm terribly out of practice. May I take a rain check on the invitation?"

"You'd better come," Mother coaxed. "Another evening may not be so pleasant."

"I'll chance it. As I say, I'm out of practice, and I need to get my playing smoother. Thanks just the same."

Out of practice! Smoother! Had he ever been in practice? Would any amount of sawing away make him smooth?

Tony went on with his alleged practicing, and Mother came downstairs. "Now I've committed us to going to town," she whispered to me. "I don't feel like swimming, but we have to escape somehow."

"You might go to a show," I suggested.

"A show costs money," she sighed, "and your father's loan from the bank is all budgeted to the last penny. No, we might sit in the club and watch the boats and the diving. Maybe your father and Eric would like a swim. Sure you won't change your mind and come with us?"

"I must make use of the wheel," I sighed. "Surely to goodness he'll get tired of practicing. But what if he makes a habit of it?"

"I'd welcome Hamlet back," Mother stated emphatically. "I'd even plant a special bed of begonias for him."

Enviously I saw Mother, Dad, and Eric drive off in the Ford. The repair work had made it run much better, and Eric had traded parts with one of his friends, and his share of the exchange was a car seat that did not have the springs sticking through. He had done some work on the back seat too, which made it almost comfortable.

"Why do I have to be so conscientious?" I asked myself.

I love to swim, and I might have practiced diving. I always used to enter for the diving events at the annual regatta. I never won, but I had the fun of competing. I went sadly into the studio, wedged a lump of clay, and threw it on the wheel to make a cup. Above my head the grating noise of the violin went on and on. Tony was trying, of all things, to play Brahms's "Lullaby." The hideous row would have wakened sleeping babies for a mile around.

I was hot, sticky-hot, and I kept thinking about the water, how cool and delicious it would feel. Very likely there would be a pleasant breeze from the lake. Probably some of my friends would be there . . . possibly Garth.

I suppose there is no instrument on earth that can produce such nerve-rending, off-key, rasping, scratching, whining noises as a violin badly played. The awfulness of Tony's playing amounted to genius in reverse. At last I couldn't stand it any longer. I put a damp cloth around the piece I was making and put it in a can. Then I went up to my room to change into shirt and jodhpurs. I stole out of the house and out to the stable for Goldie's bridle.

I hadn't seen Diana for a few days, so I rode over there. I was tempted to let down my hair and weep on her shoulder, but I decided not to mention Tony's violin. The party line is our grapevine, and I was afraid of some critical word reaching Tony's ears.

Diana was, as usual, entertaining three boys on the veranda. "Hi, stranger," she called out. "Light down and have a glass of lemonade."

I tied Goldie to a tree and went up the steps to the veranda. I could hear the ice tinkle as Diana poured me a glass of lemonade.

"Won't your horse stand if you leave his reins on the ground?" one of the boys asked.

"I never taught him that. He isn't a cow pony. He's been trained to hand signals," I said.

"Don't be so snappy," Diana reproved me.

"I'm sorry. It's been a long, hot day, and I couldn't go for a swim with the family because I had some work to do. I'll be sweet as soon as I've drunk this delicious cold lemonade." I sank into a chair and relaxed.

"I have some new dance records," Diana said. "When you've had a rest, would you care to dance? The veranda floor isn't too bad."

"Oh, I'm not too tired to dance," I said. "Just as soon as I've finished this glass."

We danced for an hour, while heat lightning played over the sky. Then I rode home through the warm, fragrant night. The house was quiet and dark.

13

Surprise

The last day of July is my birthday, and I have always had a party or a picnic, but this summer I realized that there was no money for festivities and I must skip it for a year. So I was thrilled when Garth phoned to invite me to dine at the Willow Inn and go to a good picture. I went dancing out to Mother in the kitchen.

"I didn't expect any treat for my birthday this year, but I'm going to have one after all."

Instead of looking pleased and interested, Mother looked up with a scared expression in her eyes. "What treat?"

"Garth Esselmont has invited me to dinner at the Willow Inn and a show. Isn't that gorgeous? Why are you looking distressed? Don't you approve of Garth?"

"Oh, yes. I think he's a dear, but would you invite him here to dinner instead of going to the Willow Inn? I traded some of our melons for a big young chicken from Mrs. Bray's flock, and I was planning a birthday dinner with a cake. Dad and Eric will be so disappointed, because Eric's present has something to do with the dinner."

"Oh, Mother, I had no idea . . . I thought we'd just skip my birthday this year. I'll phone Garth and ask him. It will mean letting him know it's my birthday."

"I believe he knows it's your birthday. He can take you to a show after dinner."

I was feeling let down because I had never been taken out to dinner and I could see myself in my green dress, sailing grandly into the Willow Inn, with a handsome escort that half the girls in Kelowna would envy me. I phoned Garth and explained the whole situation. Garth sounded disappointed, but he accepted graciously.

I didn't expect any presents this year, but there was a large parcel on my chair and a smaller one on the table at breakfast. The large one was a white sweater that Mother had knitted for me.

"Oh, Mother, how darling of you!" I was simply overcome. I tried it on and it fitted perfectly. Then I saw that Eric was fidgeting, and I opened his parcel. It was a large bundle of asparagus.

"For your birthday dinner," he explained.

Asparagus grows wild in some of the orchards, and Eric makes pocket money by searching for it and selling it to housewives. The owners of the orchards give him leave to take it, since they have no time to bother about such a vagrant crop.

"That's marvelous, Eric, dear," I said. "Garth will be glad he came to dinner here instead of taking me to the Willow Inn. I'm sure it will be much nicer."

That afternoon at four Lyn and Susan asked leave to stay for half an hour to work on their projects. Just as I said OK to that, Dad came to ask for my help in checking the orchard boxes to see how much lumber would be needed to replace duds.

Dad usually does that job himself or with the help of one of the men, so I wondered why he called on me, but out I went. Mother called from the veranda to come and have a cup of tea. We had tea and then went to the shed to count the boxes. By the time that job was done, I had to hurry indoors to have a bath and dress in my green nylon for the dinner that was already sending pleasant odors from the kitchen.

I wasn't ready when Garth rang the bell, and Mother opened the screen door to him and took him into the kitchen, where she could talk without my hearing her. Later I understood the reason.

Garth had brought me the sweetest corsage of pink rose-buds, which gave just the touch needed to make my dress festive. "It's the prettiest corsage I've ever had, Garth," I told him sincerely.

Mother had cooked a most delicious dinner, and most of it had come from the garden. The chicken was large and tender, and with it were new potatoes, green peas, Eric's asparagus, and a salad of leaf lettuce, tomatoes, and chives. For dessert there was a melon and a cake with nineteen candles.

"We certainly wouldn't have had such a dinner as this at the Willow Inn, Mrs. Warburton," Garth told Mother. She beamed at him. Tony was very quiet during the meal.

I could see that we couldn't possibly be in time for the early show, but Garth didn't seem to be heeding the time. We were having dinner in the screened veranda, on the east side of the house, and there was a pleasant cool little breeze. At last Mother glanced at her watch.

"If you two are going to a picture, you should be off,"

she said, and I caught a meaning look pass between her and Garth.

I ran upstairs for my new sweater, in case it should be cool later in the evening, and off we went in Garth's Studebaker. We drove along the straight road and down the winding KLO grade. Suddenly Garth stopped the car and searched in his pockets.

"Darn," he said, "I've left my wallet at your house. We'll have to go back for it." He turned at the first intersection and drove back slowly.

There's something funny about this, I thought. Why should he leave his wallet behind? Why was Mother fussing about the time? I began to have suspicions. When we stopped in front of my home and Garth opened the car door for me, I just sat there.

"Why should I get out?" I asked innocently. "You know where you left your wallet, don't you? I'll just sit here and wait for you."

Garth's forehead wrinkled up. "I might be a few minutes," was his feeble explanation. "I forgot to ask you to show me what you have new in the studio. It's only eight, so we'll be in plenty of time for the late show."

This explanation sounded so phony that I was sure something was afoot, and I decided to tease him a little bit. "I want to forget work on my birthday evening. I don't want to go near the studio till tomorrow morning."

Garth looked so upset that I expected him to break down and sob. Suddenly he thrust out his chin. "Look here, my girl, this is my car and I say you're to get out of it, and if you won't take me to your studio, I'll carry you there, kicking and screaming."

"Why, Garth, are you a cave man at heart?" I cried.

"I sure am," he said grimly. "Hop out, gal."

I do like a masterful man, though I wouldn't admit it to him. "OK, OK," I muttered. "Don't get violent. I'll come peaceably."

As we went in, I could hear suppressed giggles and hushes from behind the closed door of the studio, so I wasn't too greatly surprised when the door opened and a chorus greeted us, all out of tune.

"Happy birthday to you! Happy birthday to you! Happy birthday, dear Penny, happy birthday to you!"

I looked all around, blinking to show how surprised I was. The big table had been moved against one wall, and the looms and the potter's wheel had been put out of the way. There were flowers in vases on the mantelpiece. The canvas and linoleum had been lifted from the floor and the floor waxed. The old gramaphone and a pile of dance records had been brought in. All my class were there, beaming, even Mrs. Bellair, and also Diana and two of her boy friends, Eric, Mother, and Dad.

"So this is why you left your wallet, you scheming, conniving deceiver," I laughed at Garth. "Well, this is a lovely surprise."

"It was Doreen's idea," Lyn said frankly, "but the whole class brought the refreshments."

I was terribly touched. "How darling of you all, and especially you, Doreen, for dreaming it up!"

Mrs. Bellair stepped forward with an elegantly wrapped parcel in her hands. "I have been appointed to the pleasant task of presenting you with a small token of the affection and good wishes of your class," she intoned. "We hope you will accept it as a memento of this delightful summer."

"Oh, girls and boys, you make me want to cry!" I said as I took the parcel. "Thanks a million, million!"

I was so overcome that my fingers fumbled, and Tony had to undo the ribbon for me and disclose a shopping bag woven of black wool and lined with rose-colored silk. A floral design was embroidered on one side. Two rods of maple held the top rigid, and the four ends were carved into horses' heads. The loops to hold the bag were made of plaited leather thongs.

"We all worked at it," Tony explained. "Each one made a different part."

"I haven't deserved such a beautiful gift as this . . ." Words stuck in my throat. "I can't tell you how I value this lovely, lovely bag."

The guests from outer space had to examine the bag's workmanship and admire it, and then Pat Terry put a dance record on the gramaphone.

Instantly Garth and Tony asked me for the dance, and you couldn't say that one was a thousandth of a second ahead of the other. They stood and glared at each other. I was in a spot. Garth was my escort and had given up his own plan for the evening to fit in with this surprise party; Tony was one of the hosts and had done a good deal of the work on my bag. I knew he had carved the horses' heads because one day I had caught him at it, although I never suspected the object of his work. Which should I choose?

This was a case for Ann Landers and Abigail van Buren. I wished I could send them a telepathic question and get an answer in the same way. Solomon with the baby had a cinch. So I stood there with my mouth open, like a dumb cave woman, while those two glowered at each other like cave men.

Suddenly Garth smiled, and Tony shrugged. Tony turned to me. "May I have the next one, Penelope?"

"Thank you, Tony," I said, "and the third I'll sit with Pat and help him to put on the record."

Tony bowed in an extra courtly way, like a man who is boiling mad, and went off to ask Doreen for the dance. Garth whirled me out on the floor, and he had a self-satisfied smirk on his face, the look of a cave man who has won. Garth danced well and he was fun to talk to as we danced. Some dancers lapse into silence, as if the rhythm and music were better without words. Me, I like to chatter.

The moment Pat put on the next record, Tony was bowing to me. "You promised me this."

Tony was a dream of a dancer. Chatter seemed unnecessary as we melted into the music. He could have been one of a dance team in a floor show, although I didn't realize that at the time. It was magic—gulls swooping, seals diving, every sort of fluid motion combined with the glamor of moonlight on water. I was entranced.

When the music stopped, we went on dancing for a few silent bars. "You're a super dancer, Tony," I said dreamily. "I never danced with anyone like you before."

"You mean I dance better than Garth?" His smile was triumphant.

"I meant what I said, with no comparisons," I said rather crossly. "Why bring Garth into what was meant as a compliment to you?"

"You're right," he said gloomily. "The first and perhaps the last compliment I shall ever receive from you."

"Oh, Tony," I scolded, "don't be like that. I have praised your work heaps of times, and I think those horses' heads are the cutest things."

"Sure, you've praised my work," he admitted, "but when have you ever complimented me myself?"

"Your work is part of you, and now I must go and help Pat choose the next record."

Pat looked up with a smile of such touching sweetness that I thought, "How he would love to be able to dance." I had grown so used to his shuffling steps that I hardly noticed his lameness and only thought of his progress in craft work.

"May I help you choose a record and sit it out with you?" I asked.

"Oh, Penelope, you *are* a nice gal," he said. "Did you guess that putting on records is a lonesome job?"

"No. I just wanted to talk to you." We looked over a few records and discussed them, and then he put one on.

"I can't get over it," I told him. "I never dreamed that you were all working on a present for me. I'm going to treasure it all my life. Which part did you make?"

"I made the handles at home, and Tony carved the horses' heads. The others each did a bit of the weaving and embroidery. Mrs. Bellair sewed in the lining."

At the fourth record Garth was on hand again, and then I had a waltz with Dad, and a fox trot with Eric, and after that we had a square dance which I danced with one of Diana's friends. Mother and Mrs. Bellair had disappeared, and soon the fragrance of coffee was wafted in from the kitchen. The class had brought soft drinks, too, and sandwiches and cake. They spread a cloth on the big table and wouldn't let me lift a finger to help.

"You're the birthday child," Doreen said.

When all the others said good night and went home, Garth lingered in the hall. "How about carrying out our original plan on Saturday evening?" he asked.

"So many thrills all in one week? I'd love to go. Thanks

a million, Garth. It was sweet of you to give up your plan and fall in with the conspiracy," I said.

"Walk out to the car and look at the moon." Garth took my hand and gently pulled me out and down the steps. We walked away from the black shadow of the house and looked up at the moon, just one day past the full. The night was warm, and the air was sweet with scents of garden and orchard, with a tang of sagebrush from the hills. I was just beginning to feel sentimental and glamorous when a most unearthly noise came from above our heads.

Garth clutched my hand tighter. "What in Heaven's name is that? A cat?"

I started to laugh and felt that I couldn't stop. "It's part of a cat I believe, unless they make them of nylon now."

"What do you mean?" Garth asked. "What is part of a cat?"

"It's Tony playing his violin. Don't they make violin strings of catgut?"

"Then the cat is haunting Tony. Do you have to put up with that all the time?"

"Since Hamlet was returned to his owner. He used to howl so loudly that Tony was discouraged from playing."

"I'm not surprised. I could howl myself. I never heard such a goshawful row. I hope he'll pack it up soon and let the family sleep. I'll call for you at six on Saturday. Right?"

"I'll be ready," I said. "Good night, Garth, and thank you for everything."

The moon was merely a satellite of the earth, the air was just oxygen and stuff we breathe, and the night had lost its magic as I went upstairs and heard Dad knocking on Tony's door.

"Have a heart, son," he was saying. "We want to catch some shut-eye."

And then everything was quiet, but I couldn't sleep for some time, for the moonlight was streaming in at the open window and my mind was swirling with emotions and thrills of the best birthday I could remember, better even than the one that brought me a talking doll.

14

The Regatta

The great annual event in Kelowna is the regatta, which lasts for three days and attracts visitors from as far away as Vancouver, Victoria, and Seattle . . . farther, I dare say one would find by studying the license plates on the cars. This year the weather was radiant and not so oppressively hot as it had been. There was a breath of late summer mellowness in the mornings. In the evenings we could see the northern lights dancing near the horizon.

I couldn't give holidays on Thursday and Friday as well as the usual Saturday, so pupils just had to take leave of absence for the special events they wanted to take part in or to watch. I had kept up my swimming and diving all winter in a swimming pool in Vancouver, so I wanted to enter in the diving contests for women.

"Class," I said on the Monday before the regatta, "we must work out a schedule to let us see as much as we can of the Regatta without losing too much time from work, especially for those who are in the middle of modeling a piece."

"I'm entered for the diving events," Tony said.

"I have not the slightest interest in sports of any sort," Mrs. Bellair said stiffly. "As far as I'm concerned, you need not give a holiday at all, Penelope. I shall be here both days."

There was a sort of stifled moan from the rest of the class, with little squeaks of protest from Lyn and Susan. "I want to go to the regatta every day and all day," said Lyn.

"I'm in two swimming events," Susan contributed. "I can't come here at all on Thursday and Friday, and we don't come anyway on Saturday."

"Saturday is the only time I specially want free," Doreen murmured. Pat Terry and the two elderly ladies said nothing, so I judged they didn't want extra holidays. It looked as if I should have to keep school open and give up hope of competing myself. But I did want to see the water skiing.

"I'll be here on Thursday and Friday, and anyone who wants to work may come. Those who prefer to take a holiday won't get black marks."

Then Pat Terry spoke up hesitantly. "It seems a crime to tie you down, Penelope. You usually enter for the diving, don't you?"

I gave him a grateful smile. "I've gone in for the diving other years, but I've never won anything yet, so I won't miss much. I'll see Tony dive on Saturday."

Doreen made a sensible suggestion. "Let's get a program and see what we can squeeze in without missing the class. You might close early one day, Penelope."

"Good idea," Tony agreed. "I have a program in my room. "Excuse me for a minute, and I'll get it."

We studied the program and worked out a timetable by which everyone could work part of the day and go to the regatta for the events they specially wished to see. I couldn't make it fit the diving contests for myself, but I didn't mind very much, although I had developed a smooth half-gainer during the winter.

I had been working hard to make a good shipment of Ogopogo ware to Esselmont's store, and Garth had promised to have a display of that and other pottery done by my class. On Wednesday evening he drove out to take me into town to see the window display. I was glad to go, partly to get away from Tony's violin, but chiefly to go with Garth.

The streets were swarming with visitors, tourists, and cowboys. To my delight a group were admiring our pottery. Not all the remarks were complimentary. A boy told his small brother, "That's no Ogopogo. Wait till you see the real one in the lake tomorrow."

"Will the real live Ogopogo come to the regatta?" asked the younger boy. "I should think it would be scared of all the people."

"Not the live one, stupe," his brother said scornfully. "The big phony one they have at the regatta."

I had often seen the monster that floats in the water at these regattas, a fearsome creature with coils made of inner tubes and a head with glaring eyes. I hoped the smaller boy would get a kick out of seeing it on the following day.

When I could do so without pushing, I sidled in closer to see how Garth had dressed the window. There was some other craft work besides ours, and the whole arrangement was very attractive. Some of the other potters had apples and tomatoes for decorative motifs. They were prettier than mine, in a way, but not so distinctively Okanagan as the Ogopogo.

"You have made a grand window, Garth," I admired, which caused a few people to turn and look curiously at him.

"Let's go to Chez Louis and have a cup of coffee," he said quickly and drew me away from the fascinating window.

"I hope you'll be able to cheer for me in the water skiing," Garth said as we strolled along wide Bernard Avenue. "I'll do better if I know that you're in the gallery rooting for me."

"Oh, I will," I promised. "I mean to spend the whole of Saturday at the Aquatic Club. I want to watch Tony diving, too."

"He ought to take his violin in with him when he dives," Garth muttered.

It was still light, with the warm golden glow of the valley sunset, when we drove back to the KLO bench. On the flat land of the valley the tomato farms were red with ripe tomatoes, and the onion acres were tawny. Late as it was, the truck farmers were at work harvesting their crops. I could see people of many races bending over their vegetables: Italians, Hindus, Dutch, Czechs, Chinese, Japanese. I had often thought the annual school sports day was a junior United Nations, for they were all friends together.

A cock pheasant trailed his long tail in the dust as he sauntered across the road. The light from the western sky showed the ring around his neck and the iridescence of his head and neck plumage. In the orchards on either side of the road the trees were already bending under the weight of apples.

When the Studebaker stopped in front of the house and Garth got out to open the car door for me, I asked him to come in.

"If you'll excuse me, Penelope, I'll hurry back. I have a shipment of china to unpack, and I want to clear things away so that I'll be able to enter the water skiing competition without leaving all the work to Dad."

As it was not yet dark, I took a lump of sugar out to Goldie. Tony was sitting on the top rail of the pasture fence, just looking at my horse.

"Why, hello," I said, "think of meeting you here. I always say it's a small world." I unlocked the gate and went into the pasture.

"Don't laugh at me," he pleaded. "I like to watch the fluid way he moves and how the golden lights play over his muscles. I like to see the ripples when he shrugs flies off his back. I've noticed a number of horseflies around. One took a chunk out of me."

I whistled to Goldie, and he came at a long, flowing gallop and stopped short to nuzzle my shoulder and pick the lump of sugar off my palm with his flexible velvet lips.

"If you haunt the pasture, you must be on the look-out for horseflies."

I patted Goldie and talked to him for a few minutes and then went out of the gate and turned the key in the padlock. Tony got down from the rail and walked back to the house with me.

"I'm feeling discouraged," he said gloomily.

"You? Discouraged? I always thought you were full of bounce and sure of yourself."

"That's just my defense mechanism. For one thing, I'm disheartened because I cannot, try as I will, learn to play the violin."

I reeled from the shock. "I thought you believed you could play the violin."

"I have no ear for music, but even I can hear that I

make horrible noises. I'm not completely insensible," he said crossly.

"Then why?" I fumbled. "What makes you keep on making these distressing sounds?"

"How kindly you express it! Well, it's like this. My godfather, who is a pushover for anyone who plays the violin, promised me, when I was fifteen, to finance me for a year's travel in Europe as soon as I could play the violin, even passably. I've had lessons, I've practiced faithfully, and I can't play the darned instrument because I have no ear. I'm alert to rhythm, but not to tone. I haven't even learned to play the open notes in tune, and anyway the open notes don't occur often enough to save the day."

"Well, this is all news to me. Then, why did you seem pleased to be able to go on with your violin when Hamlet went back to his owner?"

"I wasn't really. I was putting on a show for my own benefit. One reason that I was so sad about losing Hamlet's company was that I'd have to go on practicing."

"It didn't occur to you that we might be suffering too?" I asked.

"I kept hoping for a polite request to pack it up. You're all so terribly kind. Have you been suffering much?"

I told him frankly, "We've gone out whenever we possibly could. It's probably been good for us to go about more than usual."

"You can stay home and relax. I'll sell the blasted thing."

"If your father's pottery works pays well, he may send you to Europe to visit the great ceramic plants and learn their methods," I suggested.

"That's an idea," he said cheerfully. "That would be great, fabulous, especially if I were going on a honeymoon with a girl I know."

He looked at me in a way that made it hard to pretend I didn't guess the name of the girl. Luckily we were at the house, and I skipped up the steps and pulled open the screen door. I found my parents in the living room, reading and enjoying the quiet. Tony went up to his room. When I heard his door close, I told Mother and Dad about the hopeless violin practice.

"Well, that's a lesson to me," said Mother, "not to judge anyone harshly."

"It's a lesson to me," Dad added, "never to put up with an annoyance without screaming about it."

The first event we went to watch from the Aquatic Club was the men's diving. I've learned enough the hard way to appreciate the fine points, so I enjoy watching a diving contest even when I don't know the divers. There were half a dozen in this class, and they were good.

"Tony will have to go some to beat these boys," Eric said.

Tony came last, and in each type of diving he was supreme. Gainer, half-gainer, swan, jackknife, double somersault, backward somersault—in all of them he was like a seal in the water, so smoothly, so fluidly he twisted in the air and in the water that he seemed to be made of rubber. When he hit the water, he was like a knife plunging into cheese. The water closed over him with hardly a splash.

"Boy, can he dive!" Eric was awestruck.

Eric can swim and dive respectably, but he does not enter contests. Living six miles out of town, he has not the opportunity to practice that the boys who live beside the lake enjoy.

"I wish you were entered in the diving, Pen," my

brother said. "It makes it more exciting to watch if one of the family is in the contest."

Tony won, and I hoped that would console him for not being able to play the violin and win a year traveling in Europe. What a pity his godfather wasn't a sports fan and had offered him a prize for diving!

Eric and I made our way through the crowds to meet Tony when he came out of the dressing room. "You were wonderful, Tony! Out of this world!" I was shaking his hand off while Eric thumped him on the back. "I never saw such diving, never in all my lessons in swimming pools or anywhere else."

"Brother, you sure can dive," Eric declared. "I'd give a mine, if I happened to have one, to be able to dive like that. You must have practiced a heck of a lot."

"You dive the way you dance," I went on, "smooth as oil."

"Thank you, thank you," Tony looked pleased. He was modest and subdued about his performance, with none of his usual bounce. Mother and Dad came then and made much of the hero. It was a treat for all of us to be able to praise Tony instead of forgiving him.

In the studio next morning Pat Terry was the first to shake Tony's hand and congratulate him. "I saw the diving," he said, "and I was proud for the class to have you as its representative."

"That's right," Tony's smile was brilliant. "I hadn't thought of myself as representing the class. That makes it more worthwhile."

"Mr. Lestrange is wearing a halo this morning," came the dry, carping voice of Mrs. Bellair. "I wonder how soon he'll have to take it off and put on a fool's cap again."

"Thank you, Mrs. Bellair." There was hoarfrost on Tony's voice. " 'Motley is the only wear.' "

"I presume that's a quotation," Mrs. Bellair said sharply. "I haven't time to waste on poetry."

"How odd," said Tony. "I thought all girls' schools played *As You Like It*. But maybe you didn't go to a private school."

I thought Mrs. Bellair would burst because she is always careful to impress on us that she went to an exclusive private school. I had grown so used to the feuding of Mrs. Bellair and Tony that I didn't expect anything worse would happen. How wrong could I be?

On Saturday the studio was closed, and the family went to town, taking a picnic basket, to meet old friends, watch the various events, and have a rousing good time. I particularly wanted to watch the water skiing, in which Garth was competing.

Mother and Dad went off in a small cruiser with some old friends who had invited them to lunch, so Eric, Tony, and I were left at the Aquatic Club.

"Mother has simply stuffed this basket," I remarked as we went into the park for lunch. "Let's look for two hungry people to eat the parents' share."

We found Doreen and her boy friend, and Eric invited a girl. We had a merry meal under the trees, then put the basket into the trunk of the car, and went to the grandstand to watch the water skiing.

Water skiing is exciting to watch—the motorboats cutting through the blue waves and sending up sheets of spray, the skiers poised as their skis skate along the surface, the stunts that take your breath away, the grace and rhythm as they loop around. I found myself wishing desperately that Garth would win a trophy so that Tony would not be ahead of him.

Probably Garth is kept too busy in his father's store to have time to practice like the playboys. Probably that's it. I'm sure he's just as clever as any of them. He didn't win a trophy, only a measly ribbon for third place. My spirits were down to zero until he came, beaming as happily as if he had won, and asked me to go up to a café for a cup of coffee.

15

The Ring

The second term of my summer school had passed the half-way mark, and now that the excitement of the regatta was over, my class settled down to hard work, fretful about completing the pieces they had started. Labor Day came early that year, and then Doreen, Lyn, and Susan would be going back to school.

I added up my accounts. Between my class and my pottery sales I had made three hundred and fifty-five dollars. I had helped Dad out with over a hundred and my expenses had been roughly fifty, so, I had only about two hundred dollars to show for my summer's work. I'd failed to make enough for my fourth year at the art school. If the returns from the cherry crop were good enough, Dad might be able to repay the hundred. Even then, I should have to work for my board by living with a family that needed a baby-sitter.

The only other solution was Eric's suggestion that I

should sell Goldie. How could I bear to sell Goldie? I couldn't unless I were starving.

What should I do if I could not raise the amount to go to Vancouver? I might continue teaching craft work and making pottery until I had enough saved to go to Art School the following year. Probably Mrs. Bellair, Pat Terry, and the two elderly ladies would continue taking lessons, and I might advertise again and scoop in a few more pupils. I could go on making pottery for the Esselmont store and—there would be Garth. The future seemed brighter than it had been when I first heard that Dad was in the red.

Having thought my problem through, I felt content to work on to the end of August and then see how things shaped up. Everyone was working hard. Mrs. Bellair and Tony were too busy to fight, the days were sunny but not too hot, and everything was peaceful.

Then the storm broke.

"My ring!" Mrs. Bellair shrieked. "My diamond ring! It's been stolen."

I went quickly to look at her hands, all covered with clay. "I'm sure your ring is hidden by clay. You really shouldn't wear valuable rings when you're working with clay. Look, Mrs. Bellair, there's your ring."

She had two rings on her right hand and two on her left, heavy with emeralds, rubies, and diamonds in old-fashioned settings.

"No, no, no!" she shrilled. "My large diamond is gone. It's worth more than all the others put together. It's stolen, I tell you. Mr. Lestrange has stolen my ring. He's the only one here who knows the value of diamonds and he's always disliked me." She was sobbing hysterically. "I demand that you call the police."

I was horrified. "Mrs. Bellair, you mustn't say such things. Your ring isn't even lost—it's only mislaid. You may have left it at home or on the wash basin. I think you should apologize to Tony Lestrange."

Tony had turned paper white. He was staring at Mrs. Bellair.

"I will not apologize." Mrs. Bellair wiped her eyes and tried to control herself. "Look at him. He's pale with guilt."

Tony spoke in a low, tense voice. "If I'm pale, it's from rage, not guilt."

"A man who would steal a horse would steal a ring," Mrs. Bellair asserted.

"Who stole a horse?" asked the irrepressible Susan.

"Mr. Lestrange did. Twice he tried to steal the palomino."

"Please don't be so foolish, Mrs. Bellair." I had to forget that she was an elderly matron and I a young girl. "Tony did not steal the palomino; he merely rode him for exercise."

"I demand that you call the police."

"I will not call the police until we've made a search of this room and your gloves and the powder room, and until you have phoned to your husband and asked him to look in your jewelry box, or wherever you keep your rings," I said firmly.

"You may search this house, but if my husband hears that I've lost the ring, he'll be furious, and so will my daughter-in-law. It's an heirloom and very valuable."

So we searched, and I went to the powder room and looked very carefully, and even felt with a hooked wire down the drain. I brought a broom and swept the studio floor and went around with a flashlight. We turned Mrs. Bellair's gloves inside out and made her do the same with her pocket and take everything out of her handbag. I peered into the vase she was modeling.

"Send for the police," Mrs. Bellair insisted.

"Yes, send for the police, Penelope," Tony said. "I want to be cleared of this charge."

"Yes, do send for the police, Penelope," Doreen urged. "We're all under suspicion until the wretched ring is found."

Mother and Father had gone to town, so I had no one to consult. I went to the telephone and called the police station.

"Penelope Warburton speaking. Mrs. Bellair has lost a diamond ring and she insists that I call you."

"Don't you worry, Miss Warburton. I'll be right out." I recognized the voice of the young Mountie who sometimes drops in for lunch or a cup of tea.

I went back to the studio. "The police will be here as quickly as possible. We might as well go on with our work."

"I cannot possibly work in my present state of mind," Mrs. Bellair declared and sat stiffly waiting while the rest of us made a pretense of working.

In ten minutes the constable was at the door. I let him in and introduced him to every member of the class. He took out his notebook. "You were wearing this ring when you came here this morning, Mrs. Bellair?"

"I certainly was."

"And now it is not on your finger?"

"It is not on my finger. It is an antique ring with one large diamond and two small diamonds."

"Did someone pull it off your finger?"

Mrs. Bellair's mouth dropped open. All our mouths

dropped open. Why hadn't we thought of that ourselves? How could anyone steal a ring off her finger without her knowing it?

"No—no," she faltered, "and I didn't take it off, but it must have fallen off and been picked up by someone in this room."

"Can you swear it was on your finger when you came into this room?"

"I certainly thought it was—I didn't miss it until a short while ago. I know I didn't take it off myself."

The constable put his notebook away. "Madam, your ring is lost. It is not stolen. You had better advertise in the lost-and-found columns and offer a reward. I guess that will be all, Miss Warburton." He gave me a funny little smile as I showed him out the door.

When I came back to the studio, Tony was standing up. He had taken everything out of his pockets, spread the items on the table, and pulled the pockets out. He took off his shoes and socks and begged me to examine them.

"Oh, don't be silly, Tony," I said sharply, for my temper had worn thin. "What the policeman pointed out should have been obvious. We all know you didn't go and yank the ring off Mrs. Bellair's finger. I think you should go out and search in your car, Mrs. Bellair. I have heard of rings being pulled off with gloves and then falling out of gloves. I'll come with you."

We went out to the car, and I could imagine the chatter in the studio after the door closed. We lifted the floor mat and poked in the glove compartment, and looked up and down the road, but there was no ring.

"My husband will be so angry," she kept wailing. "He wants me to keep it in the bank, but I say to him, 'What's the use of having jewelry and keeping it in the bank? It's meant to be worn, not hoarded.' "

I could see Mrs. Bellair's point about keeping a ring in the bank. If you don't want to wear a piece of jewelry, why not sell it to someone who does and put the money in the bank? If you have the pleasure of wearing it, though, you must put up with the risk of losing it.

"I'm going home," said Mrs. Bellair. "I can't rest till I look in my jewelry box, just in case it should be there. If my husband asks why I came home early, I'll tell him I have a headache, which is perfectly true."

The poor old lady was shaking. "Do you feel well enough to drive, Mrs. Bellair?" I asked. "I could leave the class for the few minutes it would take to drive you home."

"I am quite capable of driving myself," she snapped.

"Will you telephone if you find the ring?" I begged.

"Of course."

She wriggled herself into her car and started the motor. In a second or two she was speeding down the road. If the police catch you driving at that speed, you'll get a ticket, I thought.

When the class stopped work for lunch, Tony came after me and caught me in the hall. "Penelope, I'm sorry to say this, but I shall have to leave here. I simply cannot work in the same room with that old crone—not after this painful episode."

His eyes were burning darkly, and his face was still white. I thought he was taking the whole thing too seriously. "Oh, Tony, she was so excited that she didn't know what she was saying. I'll get her to apologize tomorrow. If you go shooting off home, it will make her sure you have the ring."

"I don't care what she thinks and I won't accept any apology. As it happens, my father needs me at home to help with the building of his pottery plant."

"Then we must return part of your fee and board for the ten days to the end of the month."

That would make another hole in my bank book. My hopes of art school were crumbling.

"No," Tony replied, "I won't accept any rebate, because it's not in any way your fault that I have to go. Don't worry about that aspect."

Suddenly the fire went out of his eyes, and they became misty. "You won't miss me very much, will you, Penelope?"

"Of course, I'll miss you," I said sadly, and that was true. Yet, mixed with my regret there was relief, because Tony was getting too sentimental and I was afraid he would get serious.

"Sleep on it," I urged. "Then, if you still feel you must go, I won't try to keep you. Excuse me, there's the telephone."

I rushed to the telephone, hoping to hear that Mrs. Bellair had found the ring. It was Mrs. Bellair's voice, as I had expected, but not the right words.

"Penelope, the ring is not anywhere in my home. Since I cannot get any justice from the police, I must resign from your class. I cannot work in the same room with that young man. I'm convinced that he found my ring and kept it."

"Mrs. Bellair, I'm convinced that he did *not*. Anyway, he has to go home to help his father with the pottery plant he's building."

"There, that proves his guilt," she said triumphantly. "He would naturally want to get away from here as far and as fast as he can."

"But, Mrs. Bellair, he asked for the police, and he

turned out his pockets and even took off his shoes and socks . . ."

"Ah, that was because he had already hidden the ring. By now he has picked it up from his hiding place and has it packed among his belongings."

What an imagination! The old lady must have been reading too many who-dun-its.

"In any case," she went on, "I am not coming back to the class. It is really a rather foolish amusement, and I'm bored with it."

"Well, I'm very sorry, Mrs. Bellair. Good-by."

I hung up. Now I had lost two pupils, but that did not so much matter, as it was near the end of the term. Tony had refused a rebate, and I didn't see why I should offer one to Mrs. Bellair. Maybe Tony would stay on if Mrs. Bellair quit.

Tony had gone to the dining room and was giving my parents a blow-by-blow account of the mystery drama. They had just come back from town.

"Penelope, what are you going to do about it?" Mother asked.

"I can't do anything but make another thorough search of the studio floor, in case it rolled somewhere. Tony, you'll be interested to hear that Mrs. Bellair is quitting, so perhaps you'll feel like staying on."

"In that case," he hesitated, "I'd like to finish the piece of work I'm on. I'll sleep on it, as you suggested, Penelope."

Mother and Dad were inclined to take a very dim view of the whole affair. "I feel disgraced," Mother said. "Such a thing never happened in my home before."

"It seems to me the police made very little effort to solve the mystery," Dad observed.

"That was because there wasn't a thing to suggest that

the ring had been stolen," I said. "A thief could undo a necklace, but even the cleverest thief could hardly steal a ring off a woman's finger when she was wide-awake. Besides, we all know that Tony steers clear of Mrs. Bellair."

We sat down to lunch, but I couldn't eat. I tried to tell myself it was not my responsibility, but I felt it was. Tony's appetite was as good as usual, and so was Eric's. He regarded it as an amusing mystery. Mother and Dad were eating in a half-hearted way, for they felt, as I did, that if our house had the ring in it, it must be found.

"I think you're right, Penelope," Tony admitted. "If I go buzzing off, it will give the old battle-axe a handle. I'll stay and help you search the whole place. Her fingers are very thin, and the ring could have come off with her glove and rolled away. It could be somewhere between the house and the place her car was parked."

"You've got something there, Tony," Dad agreed. "She might have taken off her gloves while she walked. After lunch we'll go out and search. I'll bring a sieve and we'll sift every inch of ground on the road."

After school hours I started an inch-by-inch search of the studio. I looked again into the small-necked jar Mrs. Bellair had been making.

"I don't know what to do with this," I remarked to the girls who were helping me search. "Mrs. Bellair says she isn't coming back, and no one else would want to finish this thing."

"Squash it up and put it back in the clay can," Doreen said. "It's a stupid shape."

"Maybe I'd better not. She'll be back to collect her things, and she may want it. I'll put a damp cloth around it until she comes. She has these figurines in the biscuit.

I don't know whether to glaze them or not. I'll wait till she comes."

I swept every inch of the large floor, and dusted into the corners, and moved everything except the heavy ping-pong table, even the potter's wheel. Outside the house Dad and Tony marked off the area of road, scraped and sieved the earth, and raked the garden at either side.

"I am convinced the ring is not in this house or garden," I told Mother.

She looked troubled. "Then, my dear, if Mrs. Bellair knows she was wearing the ring when she came here and has not found it in her own home, it does look as if someone had picked it up and kept it."

"Why, Mother," I protested, "a ring is such a tiny thing that it may be lost anywhere on the road between this house and Mrs. Bellair's. It must have dropped off her thin finger, and it's hard to say where or when."

All we could do was hope and pray that Mrs. Bellair would recover her ring and apologize to Tony.

16

Gymkhana

That evening Garth came to take me for a drive. I was in the studio, shaping a bowl on the potter's wheel, when I heard a tap on the open studio door, and there stood Garth smiling at me.

"Is it any use asking the busy girl to come for a drive? Have you been across the bridge yet?"

"I'd love to come," I accepted without any dithering. "Just let me finish this bowl—I won't be a minute—and change my smock for a dress, and I'll be ready. Find a place to perch."

Garth obeyed literally, perching on one of the high stools, and hooking his heels into a rung. He watched, fascinated, while I finished smoothing the bowl. "Is that to be Ogopogo ware?" he asked.

"I did think of putting on a blue glaze and using it for tulip bulbs," I told him. I stopped pedaling the wheel and cut off the bowl with my wire cutter.

"Excuse me while I wash my hands and change into a dress."

"Don't take time to doll up," he begged. "You look fine the way you are, and the evening is getting short."

I tore upstairs, unbuttoning my smock as I went, flung it on a chair, dashed into the bathroom to wash the clay off my hands, struggled into a skirt and a sweater, gave my hair a lick with the brush, and ran downstairs.

"Wasn't I quick? I didn't stop even to put on lipstick."

"You were as speedy as I am myself, and you look fine without lipstick." He held the screen door open for me. "Except—"

"Yes? What?"

"Except that you don't look so happy as usual. Has something gone wrong?"

"Has something gone wrong? I'll say something has gone wrong. I'll tell you about it when we get in the car."

"You intrigue me," he said as he opened the car door. "I hope it isn't terribly bad."

I settled myself, and Garth went around and into the driver's seat. I didn't begin my tale until he had started the car and was driving slowly down the orchard road.

"Mrs. Bellair has lost a valuable heirloom ring."

"Too bad," Garth said carelessly, "but her hands are always blazing with rings—she can easily spare one."

"But this is an heirloom, and her husband always urges her to keep it in the bank because it's very valuable."

A funny little smile played around his mouth. "That's what comes of a woman disobeying her husband. I still can't get excited."

"She insists that it was lost in my studio, and that Tony picked it up and is keeping it. She made me call the police."

At last Garth turned serious. "My word, that's bad! Did the police take any action?"

"No, just told her it was lost, with no evidence of its being stolen, and to advertise and offer a reward. Then the constable went away, but she still accused Tony, and she won't come to my class any more."

"The old witch! As if it were your fault."

"She said she couldn't work in the same room with Tony any more. Meantime, Tony said he was going home, that he'd never been so insulted in his life, and that he wouldn't work in the same room with Mrs. Bellair. When Tony heard that Mrs. Bellair was quitting, he said he'd think it over and decide in the morning. Mother and Dad are all upset and think it's a disgrace to the family."

"And of course you've searched," Garth said.

I told him how we had searched and how Dad and Tony had sifted the earth, in case the ring had fallen out of her glove.

"It's not your fault in any way," Garth said, "so you should forget it. Save your worrying for things you could have prevented or that you did by accident. I know you'd never do anything wrong deliberately. Cheer up and enjoy the sunset. Isn't it spectacular?"

We were driving westward. A great fan of flaky crimson clouds spread over the whole sky. The handle of the fan was the place where the sun had set.

"When I was a little girl, Mother had a pink ostrich feather fan," I said. "It was like that sky. I thought it was the most beautiful thing in the world. The moths got into it."

Garth laughed. "You women. Imagine comparing a glorious sunset to a feather fan."

"It's my childhood memory of something out of this world," I defended myself. "The sticks were carved ivory."

We crossed over the new bridge. The lake reflected the sunset, and all the world was gold and rose, except where the mountains stood out darkly and were darkly reflected in the water.

"I thought it might be interesting to drive up to Ewing's Landing and see how the road is. OK with you?" Garth asked.

"Yes, let's," I agreed, though I was pretty sure it would be rough.

It was not so bad as I had feared, and there was not much traffic. Garth drove slowly and talked of all sorts of things to keep my mind off its worries. After a while Mrs. Bellair's ring moved into its proper perspective, and I felt happy again.

The crimson clouds turned to pink, and then to strings of opals, and lastly to gray fluff. Early in the season as it was, some of the vine maples had turned red, and the mulleins beside the road thrust up yellow spikes. Beauty after beauty unfolded as we drove.

"Will you come to the gymkhana with me on Saturday?" Garth asked. "Dad will let me off for the afternoon. I'd like to take some color films."

"Thank you, Garth, I'd love to go. It will seem strange to be a spectator only."

"You're not entering Goldie in any class? No jumping?"

"No. It wouldn't be fair to either Goldie or myself, because I've had no time to practice."

"I'm glad. I don't want to have a heart attack watching you jump."

I didn't know how to answer that, so I said nothing.

"It's been a dull summer for you," Garth observed. "Very little riding, almost no swimming and diving. All work and no play."

"It hasn't been dull. It's been fun," I laughed. Was he

really so modest that he didn't know he had helped to make the summer thrilling?

The road wasn't good enough to tempt Garth to drive far, and before long he turned back and suggested we stop for a milkshake on our way through town.

The evening had been so wonderful that I had almost forgotten about that old diamond ring, but when I lay trying to sleep, the whole miserable business came back to me. Worse than that, I began to wonder if Mrs. Bellair had any grounds for her suspicion. What did I actually know about Tony Lestrange? I didn't know his family or his friends. He had done some unconventional things, bringing a huge dog to the house without leave, taking Goldie out of the pasture twice, quarreling with Mrs. Bellair almost every day. Could he have picked up the ring and kept it for revenge? Perhaps he was planning to pretend to find it in a few days.

No, he was genuinely insulted and angry. It was disloyal of me even to think of suspecting him. The sleepier I grew, the more I was worried and fearful, and when I slept I had troubled dreams. When I woke in the morning, I felt more cheerful and I was sure Mrs. Bellair had lost her ring at home or on the road, anywhere but here.

At breakfast Tony said he would stay till the end of the month and hoped Mrs. Bellair would find her ring at home, and come and eat crow. All day I had one ear listening for the phone to ring and the glad news that the ring was found, but there was no such news.

When Tony heard that I was going to the gymkhana with Garth, he grew moody. "He's going to take color pictures," I said.

"I have a camera too," Tony scowled. "Darned if I don't

go into town and buy some color film and take better pictures than he does."

On Saturday Garth came for me in the Studebaker; Mother, Dad, and Eric followed in the Ford; and Tony roared off in his Tatraplan. We all arrived at the gymkhana at different times and luckily sat in different places. Garth and I had good places with an excellent view.

There were a number of palominos, but none so handsome as Goldie. I was sorry I had not taken time to train him this summer. Garth was occupied with his camera. These very elaborate cameras have so many gadgets and light meters and so forth that they are very demanding. A girl whose boy friend is a camera fiend has to sit neglected when the tricky camera makes a third.

Garth came up for air. "I must get a picture of you on Goldie," he declared. "Why didn't I think of that weeks ago? Will you pose for me tomorrow?"

"Goldie will be honored. We'll be driving into town to church in the morning, but do come to lunch and take the picture in the afternoon?"

"Thank you very much. Oh, I must get a picture of them going over the jumps!"

I watched the jumping keenly, thinking that there was not one horse that flew over so smoothly or landed so neatly as Goldie. I wished Garth had a movie camera to take us jumping.

After the jumping there was pig sticking. The pig was a balloon tied to a flat weight, which swung from side to side on a long rope, hauled by a fast rider. The contestants in this event were cowboys and Indians on rough cow ponies, and they jostled one another as they tried to spear the balloon with their long lances. One of the riders was a girl. I didn't envy her riding in that mad scramble.

Then there were trick riders, a team from the state of
Washington, who could hang onto the tail of a galloping
horse and climb aboard, or do any wild, extravagant feat
that would be hard enough if the horse were standing
still. Their horses were beautiful, too, and perfectly trained.

"I hope I got a good picture of that one," Garth was
muttering. "I mustn't use up all my film. I have to save
some for you and Goldie."

Men were going out with hammers to drive in the pegs
for the tent pegging. The riders were walking their horses
about to warm them up and to calm their nerves. The
animals, with their satin coats fitted tightly over lean
muscles, were jumping and prancing as if they could not
wait for their turn to perform.

The first four charged thundering past, the riders leaning from the saddle with lances level. Two stuck their
pegs fairly, carried them aloft, as they cantered on; one
carried his peg a few yards and dropped it; the fourth
missed his peg entirely.

The next team lined up for the start. Then I saw a man
with a camera, flat on his stomach, worming his way out
toward the course the team must run.

"Tony!" I gasped. "Look what that silly idiot is up to
now. If he goes another yard, he'll be under the hoofs."

Garth stared. "He wants to get a trick shot from almost
under a horse. He won't go any closer."

The horses charged at a dead run. Tony pushed himself
nearer. "Tony!" I screamed. "Come back!" He was straight
in the path of the nearest horse. I stood up, straining as if
I could save him. In a second his head would be pounded
by the flying hoofs.

The rider, leaning low with his lance level, saw him
too, and swerved, bumping against the horse to the left of

him. I sank back on my seat. Tony was safe, but the team had no chance of winning; it was too late for them to get back in line.

Now I was as angry as I had been scared. "The dope! The selfish zany! Thinking of nothing but his trick shot!"

Tony scrambled back to the sidelines. He glanced up and saw me and gave me a sickly grin. I just glared.

"I hope he'll have the manliness to go and apologize to the rider and the committee too," I fumed.

Garth chuckled. "I think he'd be wise to get into his Tatra and beat it out of here."

"It'll be a relief when he packs his suitcase and goes home to run, or ruin, his father's pottery works," I declared.

Garth gave me a quick glance. "I thought he rated high with you."

"I don't know what gave you that idea." I spoke crossly.

"You're shaking, dear," Garth said so tenderly that a shiver ran down my spine. "That trick gave you a bad fright."

"I'm shaking with anger as well as with fright," I confessed. "He makes me so mad! Dad will be wild. I feel responsible for the screwball, because he's my pupil."

"He's an unpredictable fellow, but you have only one more week of his antics."

Another team swept past us, and all four lifted and carried their pegs. The four who had been put off by Tony were allowed to ride again and did fairly well. Then the gymkhana was over, and we went out to Garth's car.

Tony didn't come home for dinner. "He's probably ashamed to face us," said Mother.

"I shouldn't be surprised if we never saw him again," Dad grunted. "I should think he'd get in his deplorable

Tatra and drive home. We'll get a letter asking us to send on his suitcase."

I was wakened about midnight by the Tatra's unmistakable voice. In a minute I heard Tony coming up the stairs. He had taken off his shoes, and he closed his door very quietly. In the morning he came down too late for breakfast and had to forage for himself. We were all dressed and ready to drive into Kelowna to church. At lunch Garth was with us, and no one said a word about Tony's escapade and escape. I noticed, however, that Mother and Dad were coolly polite to him.

"I'd like to wash the dishes," he said in a small voice, "and dry them and put them away, as a sort of penance."

"I'll be glad to let you," I answered before Mother could protest, "because I promised Garth that Goldie and I would pose for him."

So off I went to put on my jodhpurs, and Garth brought his camera and tripod from the car. I caught Goldie and gave him a quick brushing before I put on his saddle, so that he would shine in the picture.

"I have three films left," Garth said. "One standing by Goldie, one on his back, and . . ."

"Is your lens quick enough to take one jumping?" I asked.

"Sure."

Garth took a great deal of trouble to have us posed exactly right, and his camera adjusted for distance and light. Goldie flew over a low jump in pretty style. "That should be good," Garth said, closing up his camera.

A few days later I saw the films in a viewer and they were excellent.

17

End of August

The last week of my classes was a time of finishing up work already started. I was trying to get the firing and glazing of my pupils' pottery completed and leaving my own for the early part of September, for I was not sure yet whether I should be able to go back to the art school or not. I should be able to pay the fees and buy supplies, but I had to find a place to board in return for services.

So much money had been spent on my training that it would not be fair or right of me to drop it without earning my diploma and being able to get a well-paid position, so that I could help Eric get his start in life. I wrote letters to friends in Vancouver and watched the advertisements in the Vancouver papers.

I was not nearly so crazy to go away for ten months as I had been. There was Garth to consider. I had to admit to myself that I was in love with Garth, and I was not sure

how he felt about me. Would some other girl lure him away
if he didn't see me for ten months? What a deadly ten
months it would be—nine months more nearly—without a
sight of Garth, for I should not be able to come home for
Christmas.

Then there was still the trouble about Mrs. Bellair's ring.
Every day she rang me up to ask if it had been found.
Foolish woman! She should have known that I would rush
to the telephone to call her if it had been.

Eric kept nagging at me to sell Goldie. "He's just eating
hay all winter," he argued, "and you need the money."

"Listen, kid brother," I said, "I have the money to pay
for my fees, and Goldie wouldn't sell for enough to pay
board for nearly ten months. I have to make some arrangement. If I have to stay home for a year and go on teaching
and making pottery, I'll go for a ride on Goldie every day,
even in winter, so stop nagging at me."

"OK," he said, "OK. Don't get mad at me."

"I'm not mad at you," I sighed. "I just want you to stop
yakking about selling Goldie."

Time was hurrying on. I would have to register if I intended to go to the art school. Every day when the mail
came I searched through it madly, hoping to hear from
someone who wanted a built-in baby-sitter for the winter.

Garth arranged a window display of my pupils' work,
with a few pieces of my own. It was a work of art, with
vases of autumn leaves standing on woven place mats,
apples and grapes in my best blue bowl, a hand-woven
curtain draped with a tooled leather bag against it, and a
group of peasant pottery in front.

"Oh, Garth," I exclaimed, "you're a real artist. You've
made such a picture of this window that you ought to take
a color film of it."

"Good idea," he agreed and went for his camera.

All my pupils were delighted to see their work so well displayed. "I didn't know I was so clever," Doreen said. "If you don't go to Vancouver, will you go on teaching? If you had an evening class, I could come."

"We saw our things in Esselmont's window," Lyn and Susan chanted, interrupting each other. "They sure looked lovely. If you do have an evening class, we'd like to come."

"I'd want to go on studying," Pat Terry said. "Esselmont has undertaken to handle my stuff at a commission of twenty-five percent."

"If I don't go back to the art school, I surely will offer courses again," I promised.

I was almost hoping there wouldn't be any baby-sitting for board in Vancouver when the letter came—to my mother.

"This is splendid news, dear. Your Uncle John has been transferred to Vancouver, and Aunt Madeline wants to know if you'd like to stay with them while you go to art school. She would want you to sit with the children very often, because she and Uncle John intend to join several cultural and service groups that hold evening meetings. So there you are. What a good thing you didn't hear from any of the people you wrote to."

So that settled it. I wrote and thanked Aunt Madeline for the invitation, with real gratitude, because she's sweet, and so is Uncle John, and the children are as good as you can expect. I hoped I could manage them.

I had plenty to do, with my work in the studio to finish and my clothes to iron and pack, but I felt so restless that I thought I would ride Goldie over to Diana's and tell her about my winter plans. However, I didn't want to go away for fear Garth might phone. It truly was a wonder my ears didn't grow out like trumpets, the way I listened for that telephone.

"I'll wash my smocks," I said to myself. "I'll need clean smocks and I can't afford to buy new ones. I'll have to make all my clothes last and hope they won't fall apart before I can earn some money."

Only one smock was dirty, and it wasn't worth filling the washer for that, so I washed it in the sink. My hands were covered with soapsuds when I heard the phone ring. Tony took the call and answered, "Yes, she's here. You're wanted on the phone, Penelope."

I rubbed a towel over my hands and went to the telephone. "Penelope speaking."

"Hi! This is Garth. I have the films I took of the window, the gymkhana, you and Goldie, and some other scenes. Would you like me to bring them out?"

"That would be just dandy. I'd love to see them."

"Then I'll be out in half an hour."

As I turned away from the telephone, I saw Tony standing in the kitchen doorway, looking doleful. "I suppose that was Garth," he said sullenly.

"Yes, that was Garth," I answered casually. "He has some films to show us."

"Did he take a shot of me making a fool of myself at the gymkhana?" Tony blurted out.

"Why, of course not, Tony. How could you think of such a thing? We were both too scared to do anything but shout to warn you."

Still he stood in the doorway, blocking me from going back to finish washing my smock. "I take it Garth has the inside track?" His voice sounded choked. "I haven't a show?"

I was sorry; I was terribly sorry, so I spoke gently.

"Tony, you're just a kid, and so am I. Go build your pottery works and think of me only as your pottery teacher, until you forget me altogether."

"You know I'll never do that," he said in a smothered sort of voice, and he rushed past me and up the stairs. I heard his door slam behind him.

How I hate to hurt anyone! Heaven knows I had never tried to enchant Tony. I always seemed to be bawling him out for one thing or another. I hoped he would go home and find a girl who would put up with what Garth called his antics. I had a sick feeling in my heart as I rinsed my smock and hung it out to dry. I knew how it would hurt me if Garth left me for another girl.

I look a fright, I thought, and hurried up to my room to rub lotion on my hands, brush my hair, and put on lipstick. I stared at myself in the mirror. It was no use asking my mirror to say I was the fairest of them all, because I knew darned well I wasn't. If Garth loved me, it wasn't for my beauty. Still and all, I wasn't plain enough to crack the glass.

Garth came with his films and his viewer, and we sat in the living room and looked at them. The three he had taken of Goldie and me were a treat for the eyes. Goldie is a color that comes out especially well in color photography. I wasn't too bad myself, smiling at the camera.

I told Garth the news about my plans for the winter. He looked as if he had been hit in the solar plexus. For half a minute he didn't speak, then he burst out: "You are! Then, by cracky, I'm going to move heaven and earth to go to the university."

The future looked a shade brighter. "Could your father spare you?" I asked doubtfully. "You always seem to run the shop."

He laughed. "Not quite that. Dad could engage an assistant. It's getting hold of the cash that bothers me."

"Maybe you could do as I'm doing, baby-sit for your board," I suggested.

Garth rubbed his chin thoughtfully. "It's worth considering," he agreed. We talked this over for a while, and he went home early to write some letters to friends who might know of a baby-sitting job.

I went on with my work of sorting out my clothes and getting them ready to pack. My heart was singing with hope, because I believed that Garth would find some way to go to the university, now that he was determined to go.

18

Wong Kee Scores

Friday afternoon was spent in packing pottery and woven pieces, cones of weaving wool, leather, and tools. We were all sad that the happy time was over.

"The skills I've learned here are going to be a real help to me in my teaching," Doreen said. "I'm truly grateful for all you've taught me, Penelope."

"We all are," Lyn said cheerfully. Susan looked doubtful. Poor little Susan! I had tried hard to teach her, but I couldn't overcome her clumsiness. She had woven some pieces that were fairly straight, and she was proud of them, but she couldn't pretend that she was sorry the classes were over.

"You've set me on my way to being self-supporting," Pat Terry acknowledged. "I'm going to miss the fun we had here. I hope you girls will come and see me some time and talk shop." Pat looked so much healthier than when he came. I think he even walked more easily.

"Oh, we will," they promised blithely. I wondered if they would remember.

"You'll have to make up a party and drive up to see our pottery plant when it opens," Tony invited. "I don't know how soon that will be."

"Wouldn't that be fun?" Lyn exclaimed, enthusiastic as usual. "Don't forget. It's a date."

Tony kindly offered to drive Lyn and Susan home with their boxes. Pat's mother came for him and his loom and wools. His pottery had all gone to Esselmont's store. Just before he went he slipped a small parcel into my hand.

"I can't ever express my gratitude, Penelope, but this is just a tiny reminder."

He shuffled quickly away, leaving me trying to thank him as I opened the parcel, to disclose a beautifully tooled leather book cover protecting a small selection of Irish poems, lettered in green ink by Pat himself and illuminated like a missal. I ran after him and caught him just as he was getting into the car.

"Pat, this is the most lovely thing I was ever given. I'll treasure it always."

"Tut, tut," he said nervously as he closed the door and nudged his mother to drive away before I could embarrass him with my thanks.

I went back to the studio, so bare and empty now, and turned the leaves of Pat's gift book, admiring each fanciful capital letter, entwined with flowers and gilded like an old manuscript. Hearing a small sound, I looked up and saw Wong Kee standing in the doorway.

"Come in, Wong Kee," I said, "and see the beautiful book Mr. Pat Terry made for me."

The delicate work pleased Wong Kee, although not entirely. He always had some critical remark to make about anyone's product. I was packing the last batch of pottery, and he was condescending enough to admire that.

"I made it on your wheel, Wong Kee," I told him. "It was very good to have the wheel."

"You go Vancouver?" he asked. "I velly solly you go away. You come home Chlistmas?"

"I'm afraid not." I saw his mouth curve downward and added quickly, "I'll come if I can."

I went on wrapping cups in soft paper and packing them in a cardboard box while Wong Kee prowled around the room.

"What he?" he asked, laying his gnarled old fingers on the cloth covering Mrs. Bellair's partly made vase. I had remembered to keep it damp for a few days, then, as she did not come for it, I had neglected to moisten the cloth.

Wong Kee lifted the covering. "Not muchee good," he snorted and picked up the vase. "Bleak pletty easy," he surmised and tested it by banging it on the table.

"Ki-yi-yi!" he cried in excitement as the vase broke in pieces. "Ki-yi-yi! Dimon ling!"

"What did you say?" I shouted.

"Dimon ling allee time lost."

I stared and gulped and began to laugh crazily. There was the diamond ring that had caused all the trouble. It must have come off Mrs. Bellair's thin finger and been worked into the clay as she molded the inside of the vase and was completely hidden until the vase was broken. I picked up the ring and ran to the telephone.

In a few moments Mrs. Bellair answered. I was almost stammering. "Oh, Mrs. Bellair, Wong Kee found your ring embedded in that vase you were making. He broke it and there was the ring."

She was so silent that I thought she must have fainted.

"Mrs. Bellair, are you there? Do you hear that your ring is found? Can you drive over and get it?"

"I, I—will drive over at once!" She hung up, and I thought she was crying.

As I turned from the phone, Tony came in at the front door.

"Oh, Tony," I almost leaped at him, "the ring is found! The ring is found!"

You never saw a man look more as if a ton of bricks had been lifted off his back. Underneath his nonchalance he had been scared he would always be suspected. "Where? How?" he shouted. He grabbed me by the shoulders and whirled me in a sort of jig.

"Give me a chance to speak," I puffed. "Wong Kee smashed that vase Mrs. Bellair was making, and there was the ring embedded in the clay at the bottom."

"Have you told her?"

"The first thing I did. She's coming for it right away."

"I hope she's prepared to apologize to me." His mouth set in a grim line.

"I must find Mother and Dad and tell them." I was just about to hurtle off when Tony grabbed my arm. "That will keep for ten minutes. I want you as witness to anything that passes between Mrs. Bellair and me. Besides, you're holding the ring."

So I was, and so excited about finding it that I forgot it wasn't in its owner's hands yet.

We heard a car on the road then, and I opened the screen door as Mrs. Bellair came up the steps. She must have dashed out to her car as soon as she hung up the receiver. I let her in and handed her the ring without a word. She rubbed at the clay sticking to it. "I must have it properly cleaned," she muttered.

Tony stood and glowered, waiting.

"I think you owe us all an apology, Mrs. Bellair, especially Tony," I said quietly. "You gave my school and this house a bad name. Then I hope you will notify the police and give Wong Kee the reward you offered."

Mrs. Bellair blinked and her lower lip trembled. It made me feel embarrassed to see a woman so humbled. "Mr. Lestrange, I apologize, not only for accusing you of theft, but also for many cutting remarks I made to you. I took an instant dislike to you because you were so bumptious."

It was like her to qualify her apology with an uncalled-for crack, but Tony laughed good-naturedly and held out his hand.

"I accept your apology, Mrs. Bellair, and I must apologize to you, too, for some impertinent remarks. It was very wrong of me to be rude to an old lady."

It was also like Tony to get a bit of his own back, because Mrs. Bellair can't bear to be considered old. They shook hands and parted in a sort of armed neutrality. Probably they will never meet again. I was glad that at least they had not parted enemies.

"May I use your telephone?" Mrs. Bellair requested meekly. She had slipped the ring, dirty as it was, on her finger. She called the police, and the newspaper, and told them the story.

"Tell Wong Kee about the reward," she said. "I brought my checkbook and pen, so I will write a check at once for fifty dollars, if I may go into a room where there's a table."

Wong Kee had gone back to his shack, so Tony went to call him. The old man came back, looking worried, as if he expected to be scolded for breaking the vase.

"Thank you for finding my ring, Wong Kee," Mrs. Bellair said, handing him the check, "but you had better not make a practice of breaking the pottery in Miss Warburton's studio."

Mrs. Bellair was back to normal.

Wong Kee looked at the check. "Ki-yi-yi! Thank you, Missee Bellair." He bowed again and again. "I save money, now I got plenty get grandson from China. Long time I save money, maybe never catch plenty. Fifty dollah makee plenty." The old man trotted away, chuckling.

"I have been in deep disgrace with my husband since I lost this ring," Mrs. Bellair said, twisting it on her thin old finger. "I suppose now he will absolutely insist on my leaving it in the bank except for some very grand occasion. Penelope, I hear you're going to the art school again. I hope you will be successful and win your diploma and not do anything silly like falling in love."

With that she swept out of the house, stately as ever. Tony escorted her to her car and opened the door for her. He came back grinning.

"Mrs. Bellair said good-by very graciously. She said she was glad I was going back to my own home, because she was afraid one of the girls would fall in love with me, and I wouldn't make a good husband."

I began to laugh and I felt as if I would never stop. "I must find Mother and tell her." I was wiping my eyes. "That old lady is unbeatable."

I went out to the orchard, and there I found Mother at the wheel of the old truck, driving from tree to tree and stopping to let Dad and Eric load the boxes of apples the pickers had filled.

"Mrs. Bellair's ring is found," I shouted, skipping across the uneven ground. "Wong Kee earned the reward."

All three turned to stare at me. "Where did he find it?"

"He broke the vase Mrs. Bellair had left half made, and

the ring was stuck in the clay, out of sight until it broke."

"How amazing!" cried Mother.

"Extraordinary!" said Dad, "I'll give Wong Kee a dollar."

"Mrs. Bellair has given him fifty dollars, so now he has enough to bring over his grandson from China," I told them. "Old Wong Kee is bubbling over with joy."

I gave an account of the reconciliation between Mrs. Bellair and Tony, and then I went back to clean up the studio. The broken pieces of the clay vase were still lying on the table, and the whole room needed sweeping and dusting. Some day when I'm earning a salary, I'll buy my mother a vacuum cleaner. No one living in a city can imagine the amount of good earth that comes into a house out of an orchard. I cleaned the windows and wheeled the potter's wheel into a corner beside the looms, where they would all be out of the way in case Mother wanted to give a dance at Christmas.

Then I remembered that I couldn't possibly come home for Christmas, and I was just beginning to feel sorry for myself when Mother called that it was nearly dinnertime, so I had to hurry to take a shower and change. After dinner I went out for a ride on Goldie. I cantered along the main road toward Black Mountain. The air was golden when I started, but it soon lost its color and warmth, so I turned back. As I came toward the house after turning Goldie loose in the pasture, I met Eric.

"You can have the use of Goldie while I'm away if you promise to ride him carefully, to water and feed him every day, and never, never let him come down on his knees," I said.

"Oh, boy!" Eric cried joyfully. "I'll have to stable him and exercise him in winter." His tune changed. "Who pays for his hay and oats?"

"Mr. Esselmont has some pottery he hasn't paid for yet, and there is another box full in the studio to go to him. You can have that money. There's hay in the hayloft, and Goldie won't need many oats if he isn't really working. Use the hand signals he has learned, keep him well groomed, and give him a bran mash on a very cold morning. Don't ever give him a drink after a feed of oats."

"What do you think I am? A moron?" Eric asked disgustedly.

I went on to the house, in at the back door, and through to the veranda, where I found Garth chatting with my parents. He rose to greet me. I do like a boy to have nice manners. I said I would make some coffee, and Garth came out to the kitchen to help me.

"Did Mother tell you about finding the ring?" I asked.

"Yes, she did, but why did Wong Kee break the vase?"

"He said it was no good, but I don't think he meant to break it. He just thumped it down, and it fell apart. When Mrs. Bellair gave him the fifty-dollar reward, she told him not to make a practice of breaking Miss Warburton's pottery."

Garth chuckled. "Was the old boy indignant?"

"No, he was too dazed with joy to listen to her."

All the time we were talking, I was dying to ask Garth if he had any hope of coming down to Vancouver to the university, but I didn't wish to appear as anxious as I was.

"So you're off to the coast next week," he said mournfully, "and I can't see much chance of a year at the university. I asked Dad, and he said he couldn't afford it. You see, he was going to take a partner and expand the business. Dad did the expanding, but the prospective partner weaseled out, leaving Dad holding the bag."

"How awful," I sympathized.

Garth took out a notebook and pencil. "Will you give me your Vancouver address, so I can write to you? You'll write to me, won't you?"

"I will, if you write first," I promised.

"It's going to be a long hard winter with you away," he grumbled. "I suppose you'll be going out with art students."

"I won't be going out, period," I predicted. "I'm earning my keep by baby-sitting almost every evening."

Mother called from the veranda, "When are you going to bring the coffee? It's getting cool out here. We're coming into the living room."

So that was the end of that little talk, and there were several ends not tied up.

I had hoped to be happy when I packed my suitcase to go to Vancouver, but when the day came and Dad and Mother and Eric came into town with me to catch the bus, I seemed to be leaving a great deal that I loved behind.

"You look dismal, darling," Mother said tenderly. "It will be only nine months, and you'll be coming home with your diploma, so, cheer up."

Garth came to the bus depot to see me off, with a two-pound box of chocolates and a stack of magazines. He kissed me good-by and helped me into the bus. When I looked out the window, I saw him standing there, looking so sad that it made me happy. I waved and waved as the bus rolled along the street.

19

Vancouver

After the long hot summer, it was really raining in Vancouver on a Thursday morning in September as I stood under a dripping umbrella, waiting for a bus to take me to the School of Art. Cars splashed my ankles, and I felt shivery and wished I had put on a sweater under my raincoat.

A car went up the street on the opposite side. I blinked and wondered if the rain had blurred my sight. I could have sworn I had seen Garth drive by in his Studebaker, with a girl beside him. Of course I had only a glimpse of the girl. I went all cold and trembly, as I tried to watch the car and read the license plate. Even if I could have read the numbers, I should not have been any wiser, because I couldn't remember the number of Garth's license.

My bus came along then, and I got aboard. I had to stand all the way downtown, and a girl with a spike heel happened to stand on my foot. I stood swaying and trying to convince myself that I was mistaken, that the rain on the window of the car had so blurred it that the man merely looked like Garth in a Studebaker of the same year and color. Association of ideas, I told myself.

All the time a voice inside me was saying that I knew it was Garth, that he had come to Vancouver without letting me know, and that he was driving with a girl, a *girl*, a *girl!* If he had been alone, I should have thought he had taken a sudden chance to drive down, possibly on business for his father, and would telephone or call at the first opportunity. But that didn't account for the girl. I had never in all my life been jealous, but now I was sick with jealousy. It frightened me that I should feel such a surge of hot anger against a girl I did not know.

All that day in school I was miserable. It was cold in the building. When I went out for a cup of coffee at noon, the rain was still pelting down, and pools lay on the sidewalks. The first hot rush of jealous anger had passed, leaving me with a dull ache, as if I would never be happy again. The more I thought about it, the surer I felt that it really had been Garth in the car and that there really had been a girl with him. I guess the only excuse I had for being such a ninny was that I was truly in love. Now I knew how much in love I was.

Having given myself a day in the dumps, I went home, took off my raincoat in the kitchen and put my umbrella in the sink to drain before I went to my room. My aunt was out, so I made myself a lonely cup of tea. All the time I had one hopeful ear cocked for the telephone. Like a magnet, the telephone drew me nearer to it. There on the telephone table I saw a note.

"Dear Penelope, Garth Esselmont called up. He is coming to see you this evening."

My heart gave a leap that almost wrecked my larynx.
The world was rainbow-colored. The girl—? It didn't matter. Nothing mattered. Garth was coming to see me.

I must wash my hair and set it. I must put on my white
sweater—thank goodness! it was clean. I must get the paint
off my fingers. All the time I was singing at the top of my
voice, "Oh, what a beautiful morning," though it wasn't
morning and rain was still running in sheets down the
windowpanes.

That evening, when Garth rang the bell, my uncle
opened the door and brought him in, so we had to meet
formally, with no more than a handshake.

"I saw you this morning, Garth," I told him after he
had answered my questions about my family and his. "I
was waiting for the bus at Tenth and Sasamat, and you
were driving your Studebaker on the opposite side of the
street."

"You don't say! However did I come to miss you?"

"You were watching the road, and the rain was a curtain.
Come and sit down." I led him to the sofa and sat beside
him. My uncle and aunt had gone to their room to dress
for the evening's outing, so we had the living room to ourselves.

"You had someone with you," I was feeling my way.
"You haven't told me how long you'll be in Vancouver."

Garth grinned, "So you wondered about the girl. I'll be
here until the summer vacation. I followed your example
and got myself a baby-sitting job. The worst of it is that
I'll have to be back on the job by eight because the
parents with whom I board are going out. I came down
just in time to register. I'm afraid I won't be able to see
much of you because I'm taking stiff courses, and this

baby-sitting job is going to take most evenings. The lady you saw in my car is the mother of the baby."

"I'm tied up too," I sighed. "My aunt and uncle go out nearly every evening, but at least we can talk over the phone, and at week ends sometimes . . ."

"On Saturday I could take you for a drive around the campus, and we'd have lunch at The Dolphins, if you like," Garth said.

"That would be heavenly."

It was just no time at all before my aunt and uncle came out, dressed for a bridge party, and Garth had to go to his baby-sitting.

"I'll be here at eleven on Saturday. Sweet dreams," Garth said, and Uncle John let him out the front door.

"That's a handsome young man," Aunt Madeline observed. "Is he your boy friend, Penelope?"

"He's taken me out several times," I said cautiously. "His father has a china store, and he's bought a good deal of the pottery I made during the summer. Garth has been helping his father, but now he's taking courses at the university to complete the units for his degree."

"And your mother and father approve of him?" she pursued.

"They like him very much," I said primly.

I was wondering if Aunt Madeline would let me have Garth here in the evening when I was baby-sitting, if he should ever have a free evening.

Friday was fine, and I was reading the weather forecasts, hoping it would still be fine on Saturday. This September was a capricious lady, and the weather might vary from hour to hour. At school Sybil Coates looked at me with mischief in her eyes.

"Yesterday you were the gloomiest sight in the city, Penelope. Why so gay today?"

"I guess the rain got me down," I evaded. "Today it's sunny again and I feel cheerful."

"Nuts to that," she retorted. "Something has happened and I think you're mean to hold out on me."

"Well, I have a nice invitation for tomorrow, and I was —I was mistaken about something yesterday."

On Saturday I woke early, and the sun was shining. I hopped out of bed, cooked breakfast for the family, and whistled through the housework. I put on my best skirt and my white sweater and was ready for Garth.

Sharp at eleven the Studebaker was parked in front of the house, and Garth rang the bell. None of this lolling behind the wheel and honking the horn for Garth. He made his respects to Aunt Madeline and told her where he was planning to take me. She stood at the door, wishing us a pleasant day, and I guess her sharp eyes were taking in the courteous way Garth opened the car door for me before he got into the driver's seat himself. I don't know whether manners make the man, but I'm sure they improve him.

"Shall we drive around by the sea?" Garth asked, as he pulled away from the curb.

"Do let's," I agreed. "I hardly ever get a chance to go that way, because the few times I go out to the university, I take the bus from the gates. It's lovely that way too, and extra lovely now the vine maples are red."

We drove down to the sea and along Marine Drive. The gardens were a tapestry of autumn flowers: pink and scarlet dahlias, crimson and magenta, orange and yellow; zinnias of a dozen colors, and masses of bright-red salvia. Looking seaward, I could see little sailboats dancing at their moorings, with gulls flashing and swooping over them. The far-off islands and mountains were pale with mists.

"We may not see each other often," Garth said, "but when we do, we'll have us a wonderful time, won't we?"

"I'm having a wonderful time now," I laughed. I was feeling so happy and gay that every color was brighter, every view more entrancing than ever in my life before.

"So am I," Garth said. "I could go on like this forever."

We toured around the fine buildings of the university, out past the fields and buildings of the Faculty of Agriculture, looked at the collection of totem poles, and went on to the cosy old inn, The Dolphins, sitting beside the sea.

"Shall we have lunch indoors or out?" Garth asked.

"Oh, let's have it under the trees."

We strolled from the parking lot over the grass and chose a table for two in the autumn sunshine, with a view of the sea and the misty islands. There were a few other guests at tables some distance off, too far to hear our conversation if we talked quietly. A smiling waitress came and took our order.

"Wouldn't it be grand if we faced each other across a table three times a day?" Garth asked softly.

"You mean if we lived in the same boarding house?" I asked, feeling flustered.

"No, I don't mean if we lived in the same boarding house —and you know that isn't what I mean."

"Tea or coffee?" asked the waitress who had come silently over the soft grass.

"Coffee, please," we both said, absent-mindedly.

"I'm going to drive up to Kelowna for the Christmas vacation, short as it is," Garth said. "Will you come with me? If the weather's good, we should do it in five or six hours."

"Oh, Garth, how marvelous! I didn't expect to be able to go home for Christmas. I'm thrilled to pieces."

"Penelope, you do know what I mean . . ." Garth began, when a cheerful shout interrupted him.

"Hi, Garth, come on over to our table and bring your girl friend."

Two students, a man and a girl, were sitting at a table not far away. Garth gave them a lethal look and then asked me reluctantly, "Shall we go?"

"Do let's," I said loudly enough for them to hear. "They'll get ideas if we don't," I said quietly.

We took our coffee cups and went to the other table, and I was introduced. After we had sat and chatted for a while, we went back to our own table to pay the waitress and leave a tip. I knew that this was a treat Garth couldn't afford very often.

On the way home I asked, "Garth, why are you so crazy to get a degree? It won't help you in the china business, will it?"

"It sure will. It's a degree in commerce I'm working for, and I hope to be able to build up Dad's business into a concern that will support two families on the profits. All this year, I haven't been earning enough to marry on. Right this minute I don't have the price of an engagement ring."

We drove without speaking for a while, then Garth said, "You know what I'm hoping, don't you, Penelope?"

I snuggled against his shoulder. "I have a good suspicion, Garth, but I'm scared to jump to conclusions."

"Then I'll speak plainly. I love you, and I hope it won't be long before I can ask you to marry me."

"I hope it won't be long, Garth," I said.

He turned his head and smiled at me. "Darling!"

All through the fall and early winter Garth studied, baby-sat, and coached a high school student. All through the same time I studied, baby-sat, and made a braided rug. It was dull work, but it left my mind free to think about Garth and make plans. Every evening he called me up for a talk. Sometimes he came for me in his car and took me to a concert or a play at the university. When I grew too bored with the rug, I painted Christmas cards. At the art school I was doing all sorts of fascinating work in more complicated weaving, more delicate ceramics, more advanced design.

Aunt Madeline had come to accept Garth as my boy friend, but she insisted that I should write to my parents for permission to travel to Kelowna in his car. I showed her Mother's reply that it was sweet of Garth to give me a lift, and that they were all jumping for joy that I would be home for Christmas.

Dad sent me a check and told me to buy myself some clothes, so I bought a tartan skirt with red in the weave and a red sweater to go with it. I bought gift-wrapping paper and ribbon and spent a few evenings wrapping my presents. I had made a vase for Aunt Madeline and a wallet for Uncle John, and I bought toys for the children.

I couldn't think what to give Garth, and in the end I had one of my paintings framed for him. Everything was fun; everything was exciting. Yet, there was one teeny fly in my ointment. I didn't like merely being engaged to be engaged. I wanted everyone to know that I was going to marry Garth. I hate these slipshod, half-and-half arrangements.

At last the day came for us to go. I put on my new skirt and sweater because I wanted to arrive looking like a million dollars—or, anyway, thirty dollars. I had my suitcase packed, and my presents for home in a carton, all wrapped and labeled. I was tense with excitement when the Studebaker stopped at the curb. I kissed Aunt Madeline and the children, wished them a happy Christmas, and out I went. In less than a minute we were off.

It was mild, with no sign of snow, and the roads were in good condition, so we went at the speed limit of fifty. "We'll have lunch at Hope," Garth said. "Hope is what we're living on, so it will be appropriate."

When we stopped in a parking space in the little town, Garth felt in his pocket. "I'm going to give you your present now, so shut your eyes."

He took my hand and pulled off my glove. I felt a ring slip on my finger and opened my eyes. On my ring finger sparkled three fine diamonds. "Oh, Garth," I cried, "you said you couldn't . . . How in the world . . . ?"

"It's on the level, honey," he laughed. "My mother sent me down some jewelry my grandmother had left me. She said it was intended for my future wife. I had a jeweler take some gold chain in payment for resetting and recutting these diamonds. Do I rate a kiss?"

I answered swiftly. "Yes, Garth, darling, you rate a kiss."

When the car stopped at The Poplars and Mother and Dad and Eric came out to hug and kiss me, I flashed my diamonds and said to Mother, "Kiss Garth too."

I don't believe there was a happier girl in the whole wide world.

H